Ramblin' Rose™

The Wire Forests of Peru

John E. Carson

Marlene R. Carson

AMI™

An Aspirations Media Publication

An Aspirations Media™ Publication
www.aspirationsmediainc.com

Copyright © 2007 by John E. and Marlene Carson
Cover Illustration: Dave Palumbo
Layout: Jennifer Rowell
Design: Jennifer Rowell and John E. Carson

LIBRARY OF CONGRESS CONTROL NUMBER: 2007932365

ISBN-10: 0-9776043-3-X
ISBN-13: 978-0-9776043-9-5

MANUFACTURED IN THE UNITED STATES

First Printing August 2007

READ THE WHOLE RAMBLIN' ROSE™ SERIES!

The Porcelain Mines in Russia
The Wire Forests of Peru
The Secret in the Arctic Ice *(2008)*
The Chinese Fortune Cookie *(2008)*

OTHER WORKS BY JOHN E. CARSON

Last Resort

For all my Ramblin' Roses...

Foreword

My name is Rose, Ramblin' Rose. I'm a spy. Well, maybe not like James Bond, but I do work for the Agency. So do my parents; they're spies, too. And my Aunt Susan, my uncle Stephen and my chauffer/bodyguard, Richard are all spies as well.

Then, there's my dog, Samson The Great, Sam for short. He's my best friend and probably the only one in our house that is not a spy.

Some of you know these things already, but if you are just tuning in to my Internet Newsletter, you'll need some background information to understand what's going on.

Now, I didn't always work for the Agency. In fact, until I was kidnapped and taken to Russia, all I knew was that my dad worked for the government, my mom was President of her own company and they called me Ramblin' Rose because I talked a lot!*

Actually, it was Sam's fault that I found out about all the spy stuff. Well, I guess if I hadn't been playing Tug-O-War with his slimy dog toy I wouldn't have slipped and crashed into the china cabinet in the first place. And who knew that one of my Mom's collector plates was encoded with some

*See *The Porcelain Mines in Russia.*

1

very important information that just had to get into the right hands?

What would you do if you knew your parents would kill you, or worse, ground you for life? I called my Aunt Susan. Thanks to her and a very special computer named, Zip, we headed for New York to pick up a duplicate.

Everything would have been great if only we weren't being spied on.

Well, you probably figured out that we finally made it home and things did work out along the way I learned some pretty neat things, too. Like who my parents really were, what the Agency does -- No, I can't tell you but you can guess -- and the truth about the crazy stories my grandfather used to tell me when I was six.

There I go, ramblin' again. Anyway, now that I'm twelve, I'm beginning to find out that Grandpa's stories weren't so crazy after all. And, as the youngest-ever editor of *The Brookhaven School for Girls* newsletter, I am well on my way to winning a Pulitzer Prize.

Well, I don't have enough time to tell two stories, so I hope I've given you enough background to get started on the current mission. If not, you can look up the previous install-ment and get all, (well, most) of your questions answered.

By the way, they call me Ramblin' Rose for a different reason now – but you can find that out for yourself...

Prologue

I remember Grandma and Grandpa's house. It was a big white house by the sea, with a white picket fence and a "widow's watch" where Grandma used to sit watching the ocean, waiting for Grandpa to come home.

"Just like the sailors in the old days," Mother had said. "Of course Grandpa wasn't on an old sailing ship. He owned the shipping company. But your grandmother used to wait up there anyway. Sometimes we would sit with her, and watch her work, embroidering fancy quilts, table covers and pillowcases. She still does beautiful work."

"I know," I had said, thinking of the handmade pillowcases on my bed and the quilt on my wall as we drove up to the old house. I was six years old, and this would be the last time I would see it, as well as the last time I would hear them both tell me a story.

We had come to spend the weekend, and as soon as the car stopped, I jumped out and ran inside. The servants were gone now. Grandpa preferred it that way. He was retired, and wanted nothing to interfere with his time with Grandma.

I remember the smell of his workshop: pipe tobacco, sawdust, and the smell of soldering wire. It was a mysterious and fascinating place.

"Grandpa, where are you? " I hollered as I bolted through the big wooden door.

"I'm in the basement," grandpa yelled up the stairs. I followed his voice as my parents unloaded the car.

The light was on, and I held the painted railing, carefully navigating the open steps.

"Grandpa. We're here." I informed him again.

"Is that my favorite girl?" he called out as I approached.

"Depends," I said." Is that my favorite Grandpa?"

"Well, why don't you come in and see for yourself?"

"Okay, I will." I said, jumping through the doorway as if to surprise him.

"Well, I'll be darned. Sure looks like my Ramblin' Rose."

"Sure looks like my Grandpa." I said, hopping onto his lap as he sat on the stool in front of his workbench.

Hugs and kisses followed and Grandpa added a warning. "Careful, Rose. Don't touch the soldering iron, it's hot."

"What are you doing, Grandpa?"

"Working on my ham radio."

"I didn't know radios were made out of ham!" I said.

Grandpa chuckled. "They're not made of ham, Rose. People just call them that because they ham it up when they talk to each other."

I didn't really understand, so I just said, "Oh."

I watched him solder a small wire into place. Looking around the bench, I noticed lots of different colored ones wrapped on little metal spools. There were yellow ones, blue ones, green ones, and red ones, too.

I looked above the workbench at a picture of a sailing ship.

"Grandpa," I asked, always curious, "where does wire come from? Do people make it? Why are there so many colors?"

He smiled and unplugged the hot iron. Setting it on a flat metal tray, he re-lit his pipe.

"Peru," he said. "Wire comes from Peru. It grows on trees in the wire forests just like bananas do. The different colors are for the different sizes, and only one size grows on each tree. It looks like a rainbow fell on the forest. The natives cut them down with big blades and roll them onto large wooden spools. Then they send them to the USA and other countries where people put them on smaller spools so I can use them to fix my radio."

I laughed. "Oh, Grandpa. You're so silly."

"Why, Rose, you don't believe me?" He looked hurt. "Remember, there is always some truth to every story."

"Okay, Grandpa. Maybe I believe you about the wire, but there is no ham in your radio."

"Tell you what, come on upstairs and ask your Grandma about our adventures in the wire forests of Peru."

I slipped off his lap as he stood up, and we climbed the painted stairway into another world.

Chapter One

"Here we go again, Sam." I said as I packed the open suitcase on the bed. The big, black Newfie sat in the door-way, his tail thumping loudly against the door frame. He had picked up on the excitement in the house, and had not quite realized what it meant.

"Doesn't seem like very long since I unpacked." I continued. Sam thumped his tail again as I rambled on.

"But this time it's different. We're going as a family. A 'working vacation' as Mom calls it. Two weeks in Peru. Machu Picchu, the Andes Mountains, great stuff for my newsletter. Of course, there will be things I can't write about, like the real reason we're going."

Sam whined at my tone. I think he was catching on. I wished Sam could go. But Mother said, "No. Sam is used to traveling for the dog shows, but the hotel won't allow him. Besides, your Aunt Susan and Uncle Steven have volunteered to watch him while we are gone."

That was another exciting thing about this trip. Aunt Susan and Uncle Steven were not only taking care of Sam, but they would be staying in our house while we were gone. Richard, our chauffeur and bodyguard would be coming with us.

A lot had happened since I returned from Russia. I was home-schooled now with a private tutor the Agency had recommended. She was a nice lady who reminded me a lot of my grandmother. At least from the pictures and all the stories I had heard about her.

My Internet newsletter went toward my English credits, and Mom and Dad had moved into the private sector with Aunt Susan and Uncle Steven, who were married now.

After my kidnapping, my parents vowed we would work together as a family for all our sakes. I felt good about it because I was included with the adults.

I missed the kids at The Brookhaven School for Girls a little, though. But I was still able to participate in home school events and get-togethers.

As I zipped the bag shut, I smiled, remembering the passwords the Agency had used: The suitcase is open, but the bag is zipped.

Zip would be coming with us again. We still had access to him and the Agency. Dad was excited about our first contract with them. So many senior agents had left or been cut that they were contracting out assignments to former agents and private agencies. Budget problems, they called it.

This trip was about computers. The new Office of Homeland Security had called for the Agency's computers to be updated. They were at least fifteen years old and needed replacing.

Something had happened along the way, and the new computers were six months late. The Agency said there was a danger that terrorists may be planning another big strike. The problem had been traced to the wire needed for the computers. Power cords, mice, and other cords were needed to run the computers for the Agency. A lot of wire was needed to replace every computer in the Agency.

We were being sent to find out what was holding up the wire. Aunt Susan and Uncle Steven would have gone, but Mother wanted this trip for us. It was a good way to get our feet wet, she had said.

I looked out my window as I lugged the big suitcase off the bed, and set it on the floor. A car had pulled up and Aunt Susan and Uncle Steven stepped out. Aunt Susan looked up at my window, smiling and waving as Uncle Steven unloaded the bags.

Samson the Great cocked his head at the sound of the car in the drive. He thumped his tail twice, and started to make a run down the steps, but whined and sat back down.

He had figured it out.

This was going to be the hardest part, saying goodbye to my best friend. I bent down and hugged his neck, feeling the stinging of tears on my cheeks. I patted him a few times, and stood up.

"Now Sam, you know I'll be back soon. You'll have lots of fun with Aunt Susan and Uncle Steven. And Grandpa will be watching too! Right Grandpa?"

I looked into the air, as if seeing him there. Wiping the tears from my eyes, I let the butterflies of excitement take over my stomach.

"Well, Grandpa, I guess I'll find out if there really are wire forests in Peru."

Chapter Two

For a twelve-year-old girl I had traveled a lot. I felt like a veteran as we boarded the plane; I was anxious to show my mother how experienced I was. They would never know how important they made me feel by including me on this trip.

Richard was right behind me. I turned and smiled at him from time to time as we walked through the corridor to the plane. He smiled back, but his face was a mixture of emotions. All the time we had been waiting, his trained eyes were scanning the airport and passengers. He was on the job! I think he was feeling guilty too for what had happened to Susan and me the last time I had left.

I wanted to make him feel better, so I put on my most grown-up face and said, "Relax, Richard. I have flown before."

It worked. This time his smile was real. Even his shoulders relaxed.

"Yes, I know," he said. "I was with you in New York. You handled yourself quite well."

This was a high compliment, and I stood a little taller as we stepped onto the plane.

Dad took the lead, shepherding his flock into first class. He was proud to be taking his family on a trip. Dad had me take the window seat, followed by mom, then dad, with Richard on the aisle seat. I felt very safe.

I had brought some reading material with me, a print-out from Zip on Peru. Once we were in the air, I started reading.

Mom looked over and smiled, proud of her daughter, and happy to be working together as a family.

I pretended not to notice, and kept on reading, smiling on the inside. I read about Machu Picchu, the Andes mountains, the Incas and the Amazon. Nowhere did I see anything about wire forests. But I did find out there were copper mines in the Andes; and copper is used in making wire.

Thinking of wire brought back the memory of Grandma and Grandpa, and our visit to their house when I was six.

I drifted off with that memory.

"Grandpa, where is Grandma?" I asked, staring at her portrait above the fireplace.

"Grandma is on an adventure, a top secret mission!" He said, his eyes tearing up.

"When will she be back?"

"She is on the biggest adventure of them all. She won't be back, but someday we will all join her and she will tell us all about it."

I smiled and looked at the portrait again. Grandma was a beautiful woman. She stood on the "widow's watch" in a long white dress that seemed to cling to her in the wind, a large white hat in her hand. Looking across the ocean, she seemed to be thinking of far-away places she had been, dark hair alive as it wisped in the breeze. She was holding an orchid.

She turned and smiled at me.

I woke up with a start. I had been dreaming. The print-outs had slipped from my hands, and were scattered in my lap, and on the floor.

Richard was asleep, as were my Mom and Dad – and half the people on the plane. I did not want to disturb them, so I collected my papers as quietly as I could, and placed them in the pouch of the seat ahead of me.

The steady drone of the plane soon lulled me back to sleep. Before I drifted off I thought of Grandma. I wanted to know more about her. Maybe on this trip Mom and I would have time to talk.

I fell back asleep, my thoughts ramblin' from one thing to another, and I had the strangest dreams! Something about a rainbow forest...

"Rose, wake up." Mother was gently nudging me. "It's time to eat."

I woke up slowly, groggy from my nap. It was dark outside. Dad and Richard were awake.

"How long was I asleep?" I asked.

"You were asleep when we woke up about two hours ago."

"Where are we?"

"About an hour from Florida, where we'll change planes for the rest of the trip," Mother answered.

Even though I had logged a lot of flight time, it was still hard for me to sit still. But on a plane, the only thing you could do was go to the bathroom!

I got up and made my way past Mom, Dad, and Richard, who smiled and let me out.

"Don't go too far!" He joked.

"Sheesh." I said, rolling my eyes, and looking incredulous. "Just be here when I get back!" I retaliated.

There is just no privacy on a plane!

I didn't know how right I was until I noticed the stewardess. She was not the same one who greeted us when we boarded the plane.

I took a chance, and when no one was looking I parted the curtains and peered into coach.

There was our stewardess. They must have switched places!

"No big deal," I told myself, feeling silly. They probably do it all the time. It would not have bothered me at all, except there was something very familiar about this one.

Of course. She was the same one who watched Aunt Susan and me on the flight to New York.

My heart began to beat faster. What should I do?

I closed the curtain and turned around, right into her.

"Can I help you, miss?" She said.

"Uh, no, I was just curious," I improvised.

"Well, the *fasten seat belt* sign just came on. Please take your seat," she smiled.

I was glad to take my seat. Richard and Dad would hear about this.

I started for my seat as she turned around, and walked toward the cockpit. She tapped lightly on the door and stepped inside. I followed close enough to hear her as she entered.

Just before the door closed again I heard her say, "I think she recognized me."

Now my heart was really pounding. I scrambled to sit back down, almost tripping over Richard.

"What's wrong, Rose?" he said, alerting Mom and Dad at the same time.

All three of them looked at me as I fell into my seat face red, and breathing fast.

"The stewardess! I've seen her before. She was the one on the plane to New York!"

"Of course she was. She works for the Agency. They always watch us. Especially now," Dad said.

"She makes me nervous. Are you sure she's not a double agent?" I whispered.

"Well, I know better than to doubt a woman's intuition. We don't want to alarm the other passengers. We will be landing soon. In the meantime I'll turn on my COM link, and Richard, use your button cam. We'll check in with Susan and Steven and have them run a check for us."

I felt better, but I didn't know if I would ever get used to the life of an agent.

Mom looked disappointed. She had wanted a family vacation. Now she just sighed.

Richard went into alert mode, and the whole atmosphere of the flight changed.

There's nothing like a whisper to get people's attention. I could almost see the ears stretching as the other passengers started to lean into us.

I felt embarrassed. Susan would be disappointed in me for blurting things out. I decided to change the subject.

"Mom, what's the first thing on our agenda when we get to the hotel? Can we go shopping?"

"Oh, great! I can see the money flying away!" Dad said, jokingly.

The other passengers chuckled a little, and the spell was broken. My spy skills were redeemed, and we all relaxed. Even Richard.

If I had eyes in the back of my head I might have seen the man sitting behind us typing on his laptop, while the stewardess left the cockpit, and walked right into Richard's camera.

The button cam was silent, and tied into Zip. Dad was typing a message into his cell phone. He couldn't risk talking on the plane, so he used text mail. True, it could have been monitored, but he was typing in code.

It was a clever code, one that looked like an ordinary message. On the other end, Susan's cell phone alerted them to an incoming call. Since the phone was tied into Zip, the message was encoded to keep prying eyes from deciphering it.

But Susan knew what it said: "On vacation, will send pictures. Let us know what you think."

"Steven, are you getting this?" Susan asked.

"It's coming through on Zip now. Why don't you join me?" Steven told Susan.

"On my way," Susan replied, leaving the kitchen with Sam. She hooked him to his chain out back and headed for Richard's living quarters.

Richard's 'quarters' were actually his house. A "Mother-in-law's" apartment, Mom had called it. It was a small house in the back of the yard next to the garage. In it was Richard's *Ready Room*, where he monitored all the security in the house, and on the property. It was also our link to Zip and the Agency.

One of the things Susan and Steven were here for was to set up 'Ready Room' for private business. Since moving into the private sector, certain links had to be removed from the system. Dad's direct access to the Agency was now cut off, and he would have to deal through a liaison officer.

Mom's business had to be adjusted, too. Susan was to go to her office and monitor the activities of the consulting firm while she was gone. Even though Mom had a second-in-command, Susan was to be her link while she was on *vacation*, relaying any problems her second needed help with.

All of this was being done according to protocol. It was designed to look natural, and not arouse suspicion. the Agency still valued Mom and Dad's contribution. Aunt Susan and Uncle Steven were in business with Mom and Dad, so it was a working vacation for them as well. They were excited about our first contract with the Agency.

Besides all that, they were building a new house in Connecticut, and needed a place to stay.

More cover.

Susan opened the door of the *Ready Room*. "Anything yet?" She asked as she took the swivel chair next to Steven in front of the monitor.

"A picture of the stewardess from Richard's button cam. Very pretty."

Susan punched him in the arm.

"Ow! I was only kidding!"

"I wasn't." Susan said.

"I've sent it to the liaison. Waiting for a response."

A minute later Zip began to talk. "Kathy Lee Swanson, a.k.a. Kathleen Swanson, nickname, Kathy Lee. Agency operative. Current assignment; notify airlines when operatives are on board, inform captains, and monitor passengers for suspicious behaviors. No prior suspicions or outside activities. Considered safe.

"Well, that's a relief," Susan said.

"They are still in flight," Steven noted. "Zip, send a green light to inquirer."

Zip complied, and a small green light flashed in the corner of Dad's phone. He looked over and smiled.

I knew it was all right and we would all talk later.

"Nice work, Rose," he said, pretending to look at the airline magazine crossword I had started.

I smiled inside and out. This was high praise indeed!

I still hadn't noticed the businessman behind us who was still silently typing on his laptop.

Richard relaxed a little and looked over at the crossword puzzle I had started.

"I think that's 'lure' you're looking for. Four letters for attracting fish. I know that one! Looking forward to doing some of that on this trip!"

"Thanks, Richard, but I would have gotten it. Even a child could figure that one out."

Richard was a fisherman. He loved to camp, fish, and even hunt. I didn't like him when he hunted, so he never told me when he did. On this trip he was looking forward to fishing on the Amazon. He had heard of Red tail catfish that sometimes grow to one hundred pounds! There were guided fishing tours, and he was going to take one.

"Well, we all know you are not a child! It won't be long before you won't be able to open child-proof containers, or program VCRs," he kidded.

"Sheesh! I hope I never get like that! That's why people keep having kids, eh?"

"That's why some of us never grow up, either!" he smiled.

I liked Richard's smile. He was a big man, six-foot-two and about 220 lbs. With his short, dark hair and blue eyes I always wondered why he wasn't married. I used to tease him about Susan because I thought they made a good match.

"Then you could be my real uncle!" I'd say.

"And I'm not now?" He looked hurt

"Of course you are! I only have two!"

That was before Steven. Of course, he was only an uncle by marriage.

"Relax, Richard. No one could ever take your place!" I had told him after the wedding.

My other uncle was Dad's brother, Matt. He was a captain in the Coast Guard. He lived with my aunt Rebecca and my cousin Abigail in Fairbanks, Alaska. We never get to see them much.

There I go ramblin' again. Anyway, Richard liked to go the gym and work out. He stayed in shape. I knew he had girlfriends, though. One from the gym he would go jogging with and one he liked to go fishing and hunting with when he had time off.

Richard said he was never interested in Susan, but I think he was.

"Fly," Richard said.

"What?" I asked.

"One type of fishing, three letters," he said, pointing to the puzzle

"Oh, thanks!" I said, shaking off my daze, and returning to the puzzle

"It's a theme," he said. "Every word relates to flying and fishing trips."

"Yes, that's what the title says," I chided, pointing to the top of the page.

"Oh, thanks," he said, pretending to blush.

"See," I said, "what would grown-ups do without kids?"

"I do fine, besides, you are not a kid."

"And you are not a grown-up!" I reminded him.

Mom had been quiet the whole time. Now she laughed. "Oh, you two! You both act like a couple of juveniles!"

I looked at Richard and smiled. He winked back.

Dad looked over at the two of us and sighed. "We can't take you guys anywhere!" But his eyes were smiling.

Richard beamed at his only family.

High praise indeed!

Chapter Three

When the stewardess returned with the drinks, she handed them to Richard who passed them across. I got 7-Up. I felt better knowing the Agency had checked her out.

Each one had a napkin underneath. On one of the napkins was a note. It said, "The man behind you is using a laptop. Typing in your descriptions. We will be landing soon, I suggest you check him before we close communications on board."

Richard passed the note to Dad who immediately hit the Zip button on his cell phone. Richard stood up to stretch and snapped a picture of the man. The picture went straight to Aunt Susan and Uncle Steven who ran it through the liaison at the Agency.

Dad's phone showed a text message. "Might take your time. Call you later."

I had read the note as it went across, and was dying to turn around and look at the man. I knew I could not act suspicious, so I fought the urge. But suddenly I had to go to the bathroom again.

"Richard, let me out. I gotta go again!"

"Kids on planes!" he pretended to grumble. He knew exactly what I was doing.

When I returned I stole a glance at the man. He looked like any other businessman. Older than my parents, though. He had brown business-like hair, and a dark, pinstripe suit. There was a briefcase on his legs. I wondered who he could be, and why he was typing our description. He wasn't with the Agency, or Kathy Lee would not have warned us.

Mom looked worried, too. She knew we would have to wait. Everybody's mind had the same question; who knew we were going on this trip, and why did they care?

The answers finally came when we switched planes. While we were in the airport Zip called with a message.

"Alex Bacon. Vice President of Porcel-Art. Suspected of ties to hard-line communists, listed as company to avoid. E-mail tracked to Peru. Be on guard. Look for your friends at Lima airport."

"I know him!" Mom said. "At least, I know *about* him! He was named on the plate we were to deliver when Rose and Susan were kidnapped!"

"But what's he doing here?" Richard asked.

"I think I know," Dad said. "I think they have ties to terrorist organizations, like Shining Path in Peru. They also have links to Columbian drug lords. When I announced our retirement in New York, we did not allow pictures. We've always tried to keep our identities secret. But they do know who we are. I'm betting they don't know what we look like in Peru, but someone knows we're coming. Our cover is a family vacation, but someone is worried we'll find out what's going on. That wire is being held up for a reason. Someone does not want the Agency computers updated."

"Why did the Agency take the contract with the Peruvians in the first place?" Richard asked. "They could have gotten the wire from anyone."

"Two reasons," Dad continued, "First the budget. They offered it to the Agency at half the price of other suppliers. Second, their offer raised a lot of flags and the Agency was very interested in their reasons."

"So, why didn't they go to a back-up when the Peruvians didn't deliver on time?" Richard was asking dad.

Dad continued. "Well, they paid cash for the wire. Half up front and half on delivery. It would be a large sum to write off and pay again to someone else. When Huntsville called and said the wire was late, and they would not be able to deliver the computers on time, the Agency waited as long as they could before looking for options. No one was anxious to tell the president until they had all of the facts. He's been under a lot of pressure about coordinating intelligence. Most of the experienced agents are gone or scattered around the world fighting terrorism, so they contacted us. Someone in the Agency is leaking information to the terrorists, or they are getting very good at watching us."

Mom was nodding the whole time. Her company not only kept track of other companies' performance, but also kept tabs on industrial spying and illegal activities for the Agency.

"Okay, so what do we do now?" Mom asked.

"We stick to the plan. Dad responded to Mom's question. Let the answers come to us. We spend the first week posing as tourists and nosing around. If all goes well, we spend the second week on a real vacation, somewhere nobody knows. Keep the COM links on. The Agency will keep eyes on us and Susan and Steven will also."

"Dad, why are we talking here? Isn't it risky?" I asked

"Yes, but not as risky as the next plane or the hotel."

Richard nodded. Under his breath he said, "There go the red-tailed catfish."

"Don't give up so easy, Richard. This is our first private contract. We can't quit now," Mom argued.

Dad interrupted Mom. "Any time we get into trouble the Agency will pull us out. Just don't leave Rose alone, or be alone yourselves."

"That's going to be a little hard sometimes, dear," Mom reminded him.

"Yeah, well, as little as possible, anyway." Dad shot Mom a look.

I was excited and disappointed at the same time. Here we finally get to take a vacation, and we are on the job. My thoughts of getting out on my own were flying away. I had felt like a prisoner in my own house ever since I came home from Russia. I wanted to show my parents they did not have to watch me every second. And poor Richard hardly ever got any time off since I've been home.

But still, it was great knowing what was going on for a change. And we were going to a different country. This would be good for my newsletter – and my schoolwork!

"One thing is in our favor," Richard said. "They won't risk hurting us. Their plan obviously has something to do with timing. They won't risk the Agency's wrath, and spill the beans. They sure don't want attention ahead of schedule."

"Right," Dad said. "If anything, they will throw us red herrings to keep us off track. Our 'friends' will meet us in Lima, and we'll finalize our plans. The worst thing we can do is to look too worried."

Dad looked over at me. Now, he did look worried! "Rose, if you want to cancel the mission, we will."

"Are we any safer at home?" I asked my dad. "Will we ever be? We need to do this. Other people need to know someone is doing something about this so they can take trips with their families," I said bravely.

"Yes, but you should have a normal childhood," Mom was choked up. "We should not expose you to all of this. You are so young."

"What's normal, Mom? Not knowing anything about the world, and getting kidnapped on the way home from school by some pervert like some 'normal' kids I know? I see the news, too. People don't give enough credit to their kids. I'm not six any more. Was the world any safer when you were kids?"

I was angry. Angry at the world. Angry at terrorists and anything else that kept people from enjoying life. I had done some reading about Peru and knew half the population lived in poverty or barely survived. I had read about shantytowns and poor farmers surrounding a wealthy city where people went to the theater and opera. I had read about the gold in the mountains and the poor fishermen.

And I was angry with my parents for not understanding I understood. Sheesh.

The rest of the trip, Mom talked about what we would do on our *vacation*.

We would be landing in Lima, the capital city and going to our hotel. Mom had laid out our itinerary, and said, "We will not spend the whole time working."

The list of events included sightseeing, museums, the theater, the zoological gardens, Machu Picchu, and we would see the oldest university in the western hemisphere, The National University of San Marcos, established in 1551.

We also had to dress for dinner. I had to pack a lot heavier than I did on my last trip. Mom also wanted to see me in a dress! Sheesh! I wanted to spend the whole time in shorts. The climate was hot and dry. Lima did not get much rain. And besides that, I hated dresses. Give me a pair of shorts or jeans any day.

"What about the mountains?" I asked. "Won't we be seeing them?"

"It will be hard not to see them," Richard said. "They run from north to south through three countries."

"I read about the Andes. They have the second highest peak in the world. They are also steeper, and more rugged than the Rockies," I said, anxious to show off my knowledge.

"They are so high they disrupt communication," Dad added.

"Of course we'll see them. The Central Railroad offers a tour."

The more we talked about the trip, the more excited we got. Soon everyone in first class was leaning into us, listening. I thought we'd have to take them all with us.

Richard would have loved that.

Finally we were talked out, and settled in with our thoughts. Still excited, I picked up the printouts and started reading them again. I was already planning my newsletter.

Mom tapped me on the shoulder. I turned as she smiled at me and said, "And we're going to do some shopping!"

Chapter Four

Richard was back in his 'agent' mode the rest of the trip, and we couldn't wait to land at the Jorge Chavez airport in Lima.

Our 'friends' were there to greet us. Posing as a tourist agent and driver, a man and woman greeted us by the luggage carousel.

I was the tip-off. "Two men, a woman and a twelve-year-old girl." They had been told.

As we picked up our luggage ,the woman approached us.

"Your suitcase is open," she said as Mom picked hers up.

"But the bag is zipped," Mom replied.

The woman smiled, and waved to her companion. He was smiling too.

"Welcome to Peru. Peru Travel Service at your service. Allow me to take your bags. I am Rico."

"And I am Gloria, your travel guide. Please follow us to the car. I have your itinerary all prepared."

Rico stacked the luggage on a cart, and we all followed Gloria to the parking lot.

They brought us to a renovated taxi with a sign on the top that said Peru Travel Service. Rico began loading our bags into the trunk, he could only fit three of the large bags in and the two wardrobe bags, so he tied the last large bag to the top of the car, and Mom, Dad, and Richard had to each hold a small carry-on in their laps.

There was just enough room in the old yellow cab, and I had to sit up front with Rico and Gloria. At least I got the window seat!

Gloria was about Mom's age, and had long dark hair. She was Latin, and I thought of Gloria Estefan

Rico was about the same age as Richard. He wore a bright red printed shirt. He was smiling and friendly, but I could tell he was an agent underneath.

I liked them both.

"We will drive you to your hotel; there you can pick up your rental car. There are maps in the glove compartment, and all the directions you need to various points of interest. Also you will find directions to the Government Center, and the names and offices of anyone involved with manufacturing. You can reach us through Zip should you need anything. We need to maintain our cover so please remember to communicate with us in terms of travel agents."

Rico wheeled the now crowded and uncomfortable car through the streets, and I looked around at the low buildings. Most of them seemed to be from one to three stories. It was a lot different than Steven's cab and the skyscrapers of New York City.

Still, Lima was big, about 390 square miles. Rico pointed out the Zoological Gardens and the National Library. Not quite the tour guide that Steven was, but he was still proud of his city.

We were quiet most of the ride, listening to our new friends.

"The Agency does not want us to clock a lot of time on this. We will be here if you need help. Our current assignment is to track members of Shining Path. If you find a connection, of course things will change," Rico said as we wheeled up to the Lima Hotel.

It was a bright sunny day, and we were one of several cabs loading and unloading in front of the busy hotel. Rico unloaded our bags, and set them on the sidewalk.

"Here are the keys to your car. We can be reached by Zip. Good luck, and have a nice vacation!" Gloria said.

They drove off, leaving us standing by the luggage.

"I'll go in and register," Dad said, "I'm sure they will have someone to help us with our bags."

Dad went inside, and we expected a uniformed bellhop to appear and help us with the luggage.

Instead, a young boy about my age came out, pulling a large cart with a bar across the top. He was about my height, and had brown hair hanging on his forehead like it had been cut with a bowl. Dark brown eyes smiled at us. His teeth were white against his tan skin.

"Welcome to the Hotel Lima. I am Paolo. I will take your bags."

Paolo loaded the luggage onto the cart, and hung up the wardrobe bags. He seemed to struggle a little to pull the cart up the slightly tilted sidewalk and through the door. Richard started to help him but changed his mind.

"Do you really work for the hotel?" Richard asked him.

"I work for tips. I am a businessman, self-employed," Paolo announced with pride.

"I see," Richard replied, "an entrepreneur."

Dad turned as the noisy cart led the procession right up to the counter.

27

The desk clerk smiled at Paolo and winked as he handed the room keys to Dad.

"You are in 301 and 303. Paolo will show you the way," he said in an official-sounding voice.

Paolo beamed at the recognition. He worked all over Lima to help his father and grandmother.

He led us past the tropical plants and the gold ashtrays to the elevators, pulling the heavy cart across the deep carpet.

He pushed the button, and waited patiently for the elevator to arrive, trying not to look winded.

When the 'ding' sounded, the doors opened, and he resumed his work. Silent on the way to the third floor, he looked away shyly whenever our eyes met.

The cart rumbled down the hallway over the thinner carpet, and we arrived at the end of the hall.

Dad opened the door, and Paolo followed us inside. "Ladies and gentlemen first." Dad quipped.

Unloading the bags from the cart, Paolo sat them on the floor and waited.

Usually, my father was not a big tipper, so we were surprised when he handed Paolo a twenty-dollar bill.

We held our questions as Paolo took the money with an even larger smile than he already had.

"Thank you, sir. If there is anything you need during your stay, just send for me."

Paolo stuck the bill inside his white pants, and pushed the cart through the open door.

We listened as it rumbled down the hallway and closed the door, then turned our attention to Dad.

"Well, he's a hard-working kid. Besides, it's on the expense account," he defended the tip.

"I hope I'm on the expense account!" I said as Mom hugged him, and Richard smiled.

"Sorry, Rose. We're tapped out," he teased.

"Sure, Dad. You know, I left my money at home. I guess I won't be able to buy you a souvenir! Darn!"

Dad looked hurt. "I guess we're even, then. I hope Paolo knows where the McDonald's is!"

"Okay, you two! Let's get unpacked. Speaking of food, I am hungry. Where is the local McDonald's?" Mom said.

Room 301 and 303 were adjoining suites. Richard got one all to himself. I got an extra bed in the living room in ours. At least we had two bathrooms.

"Can we really eat at McDonald's?" I asked hopefully.

"No, I don't think so, Rose. It was a long trip, and I know we are all tired. We will dress for dinner, and eat in the hotel." Mom's voice was stern.

"You're not going to make me wear a dress, are you?"

"Of course, dear. You are a young lady, and you should dress like one."

"Oh, Mom! What's wrong with what I'm wearing?"

"Shorts and tank tops are fine for traveling, but this is a nice hotel. We will be seen as a family and dress accordingly."

Richard edged away as I rolled my eyes. I hated it when Mom got started on my dressing like a young lady. True, I usually wore jeans, Reeboks, and a ball cap with my ponytail stuck out the back, but what was wrong with that? Dad didn't mind.

"It won't do any good, Rose," Mom said, sternly. "I know all your arguments, but I'm still the mom."

"So there!" I finished. "Okay, but I get the shower first."

I grabbed my bag and headed for the big bathroom. If I had to dress up, they could use the small one. This was going to take some time!

I felt small in the big room. There were two sinks. Lots of fancy tiles surrounded the huge mirror, and the shower had glass doors. I made sure to lock the door.

"They want grown up, I'll show them grown up!" I said to myself. "Sheesh!"

I really didn't mind the dress. I had picked it out. If I had to wear one, I wanted to choose it. I tried to find one as grown up as possible without angering Mom any more than I had already done. What does a twelve-year old wear to look grown up? After putting Mom and the sales lady through every dress on the rack, I finally settled on my first choice.

It was blue and had short sleeves with white ruffles with a square neck and pleated skirt worn over white tights. Mom smiled in relief. I had passed up some pretty wild outfits!

Wait 'till they see me in makeup!

While I was getting ready, Mom and Dad were struggling in the smaller bathroom.

I smiled at the commotion, but knew if I was to have any freedom on this trip I would have to please Mom. She was so afraid something else would happen to me since my unplanned trip to Russia. I had to show my parents and Richard I was okay and could be trusted.

I wanted to know more about Paolo, too. Here was someone my own age – and he was cute, too!

The rumbling in my stomach was embarrassing as I stood before the mirror, looking at the new me. Now I didn't care where we ate!

An older, prettier Rose looked back at me. The ponytail was gone, replaced by long strawberry blonde hair, slightly curled above the shoulders and on my forehead. The barrette went to the hair on my right side, above my ear.

Secretly it was a COM link, Dad had said no one would suspect it. Plus, I would never get separated from it as I had with my jacket in Russia.

I wanted to show him I was wearing it.

I had gone easy on the makeup, not wanting to scare Dad and Richard. Just some blush, and a little mascara.

I slid on the black, shiny shoes and picked up the matching purse.

"Ta-Da." I said as I finally opened the door, and stepped into the living room.

"Oh my…" was all Mom could say.

Dad was in shock. "Can this be my Ramblin' Rose?"

"Depends," I said, "can this be my Dad?"

Richard opened the door from his room, and stopped suddenly.

"Who are you – and what have you done with Rose?" he teased.

I smiled as Dad linked arms with his two girls, and Richard followed behind to the dining room.

My plan was working perfectly.

Chapter Five

I felt pretty special as we walked into the hotel dining room. At first I thought we would be too formal. It was summer here and we were on vacation!

Dad and Richard had both worn suits with bright-colored ties. Mom was wearing a white summer dress. About half the people there were dressed up, and the other half wore Hawaiian shirts.

Still, I hadn't been dressed this fancy since I had worn Anna's dress in Russia. Mom was pleased, and both Richard and Dad treated me extra special.

In the dimly lit dining room, surrounded by adults, I almost felt like one. It was scary!

I looked around the other tables but did not see anyone else my age. I began to think I would spend this trip as a prisoner of grownups!

The menu didn't help, either. Seafood. Fancy dinners I could not pronounce. Sheesh!

"Rose, what would you like?" Mom asked.

"McDonald's" I shot back, and then softened up a little. "How about chicken?"

"You know we didn't come this far for McDonalds. Yes, they do have chicken. I'll order for you," Mom said.

"And a Coke." I added. Something to look forward to.

"Okay. I know this probably seems boring to you, but it means a lot to your Dad and I."

"I'm sorry, Mom. Guess I've been acting like a kid again," I said.

"We wouldn't have you any other way," Dad said, smiling.

While we waited for the food we listened to music by a local band walking around the tables playing guitars and maracas.

It was fun, and one of them stopped by our table, and played for me. I blushed.

While we ate, we discussed our plans for the week. Next week we would go to Machu Picchu. Mom wanted us to go as a family.

And Richard wanted to go fishing in the Amazon. We would drop him off at Cuzco, the ancient capitol of the Incas. There he would hook up with a fishing guide.

"But what about Rose?" he asked.

"Rose will be with us, Richard. You deserve a vacation. Take the fishing trip. We can stay in touch with you through the COM link. Rose will be wearing hers all of the time," Dad told him.

"Yes, Richard. Have a good time; we'll meet up in a few days. After tomorrow we will start our *research*, " Mom said in code.

I was getting excited again. Machu Picchu. Ancient cities! The Amazon! I had done some research of my own. This was a fascinating part of the world. It was already interesting to think there was snow back in Minnesota, but it was summer here. Being in the southern hemisphere was like being upside down. This was going to be fun!

"And tomorrow, Rose, you and I are going shopping in the Plaza."

Dad rolled his eyes, "Maybe I should not have tipped that young man so well, after all."

I smiled thinking of Paolo. I sure hoped I would get to see a lot more of him.

Later that night, Mom sat on the edge of my bed. I knew she wanted to talk.

"I just finished saying goodnight to Sam," I said. "I miss him."

Mom winced, remembering how Sam laid on my bed, and moped while I was gone.

"Yes, I miss him, too," she said. "At least he has Aunt Susan and Uncle Steven to keep him company."

I decided to change the subject, "I can't wait to see Machu Picchu!"

"There's a special reason I wanted us to go there, you know," Mom said, glad I switched topics.

"What?" I asked.

"That's where your Grandma and Grandpa met."

"Tell me about it, please?"

"I will, tomorrow. Now it's time to sleep. We'll need our energy." Mom said as she kissed my forehead.

"Great. How do you expect me to sleep now? I'm too excited as it is."

"Well, we don't have to get up that early. Gloria and Rico are going to be our guides. They'll be here at nine."

"This ought to be real interesting. You sure they won't drive off on us?"

"No, they won't. Now go to sleep. Breakfast is at seven-thirty."

"Sheesh! Some vacation! Can't even sleep late!" I grumbled.

Mom just smiled, and shook her head as she walked away.

"Good night, Rose."

"Good night, Mom."

The last light switched off, and I laid in the moonlit darkness thinking of the coming day. I was anxious to hear the story of how my grandparents met. Knowing Grandpa I shouldn't have been surprised it would have been in a place like Machu Picchu!

As I drifted off, I remembered his story about the wire forests. Soon I would find out how much of it was real.

I could almost see him standing there, smiling as he read my thoughts.

"Good night, Grandpa," I said softly.

"Good night, Rose," he whispered back.

chapter Six

"Rose, time to get up," Dad's voice brought me out of the wire forests I'd been dreaming about.

"What time is it?" I mumbled with my eyes still shut.

"Six-thirty. Breakfast in the dining room at seven-thirty. Thought you'd like to have some time together before I leave."

"Where are you going?" I asked, sitting up half-awake.

"I'm taking Richard to the airport. He's flying to Cuzco for his fishing trip. Then, while you and Mom are touring the Plaza, I'll be doing some investigating."

"Can't I go with you, Dad? I am an experienced agent, you know."

"I know you are, Rose. That's why I need you and Mom to tour the Plaza. Get a feel for the town and watch for our friend from the plane. If we split up, it will be harder to watch us."

"Oh, I know, like decoys," I said, fully awake now.

"Now you've got it. I'll be posing as a businessman, and talking to government officials. Our cover is a family on vacation. You are an important part of the team."

I knew Dad was right. I didn't like being a decoy; I wanted to do something more important, but I knew it was a very important part of the operation. We can't all be captains.

"Besides, your Mom is looking forward to spending time with you, too."

And maybe I'll get to see Paolo, I thought.

At seven-thirty we were all seated in the dining room. Mom and I were casually dressed, as was Richard.

"What's on your mind, Richard?" I asked, noticing his face as he stared at the menu. He was always on duty.

"Nothing, as usual," he kidded.

"Well, you're a bad liar," I kidded back. "Ouch!" he said. "Actually, I was wondering how you're going to get along without me. Who's going to keep the boys away?"

"Maybe that's exactly why you should go fishing." I said, drawing a sharp look from Dad. He seemed to age right before my eyes.

Mom smiled. "Men!" she said, "Sheesh!"

"Actually," Dad piped up, "they will be watching for four of us. It will help our cover if we split up even more. Besides, we have our guides, Rico and Gloria. They will keep an eye out for us too. And, they know who to watch for. Keep your COM links open, and we'll be fine."

"Yeah, you men go do your macho stuff. We girls can take care of ourselves. We're just going shopping in the Plaza," Mom said as she closed her menu.

"Yeah, we'll be fine." I agreed, trying to put Richard at ease. I wanted him to enjoy his fishing trip.

"Okay, so you don't need me," he sniffed. "Who needs to be needed anyway?"

"Of course we need you!" Dad said with compassion. "You're paying for breakfast!"

We all laughed, and dug into our food – but inside we knew we all needed each other.

At nine a.m., Gloria and Rico's car pulled up outside of the hotel.

"That's our cue. Phase one underway," Dad said, getting up from the table.

We left the restaurant and split up, Dad and Richard in the rental car while Mom and I climbed into the converted cab of the Peru Travel Service.

"So far, so good," I winked at Mom in the back seat. None of us had seen the man at the table by the window, parting the curtains to watch us as we drove away.

Our city tour of Lima began with our trip to the Plaza. Actually it was known as the Plaza de Armas, which, Gloria informed us, has been declared a World Heritage site by UNESCO. Running along two sides were arcades with shops, Portal de Escribanos and Portal de Botoneros. In the center of the Plaza was a bronze fountain dating back to 1560. Also in the Plaza was the cathedral.

"Note the splendidly carved stalls and the silver covered altars. Also, the fine woodwork surrounding them," Gloria said, like a true tour guide.

"The mosaic-covered walls bear the coats of arms of Lima and Pizarro," Rico spoke up. It was important for us to act like tourists. It wasn't hard to do, especially being surrounded by the beauty of the cathedral. I took notes, and put them in the light nylon backpack I had worn today.

Other tour groups were beginning to arrive, and we moved on to the Archbishop's Palace. This was famous for its Sicilian tile work and paneled ceiling. I was most interested in the catacombs under the church and monastery.

"That was quite a tour." Mom said, putting away her camera. "Got some great shots!"

"Maybe I can use them for my newsletter," I said, putting away my notebook.

"Sure can," Mom said.

"Can we leave you to do some shopping in the Plaza? We have another group this morning. Rico says the Plaza looks good today," Gloria said in code.

"Of course. Rose and I can handle the shopping ourselves," Mom laughed.

We headed for the shops.

"Charge!" we said in unison as we watched Rico and Gloria drive away.

Chapter Seven

It was easy to get carried away as we walked up one side of the Plaza and down the other, stopping at every shop catching our eye. We agreed not to buy too much – because it would be hard to carry everything. My backpack grew heavier and heavier as the 'not too much' piled up. Soon I was sweating in the afternoon sun, and we sat down at a sidewalk table for a light lunch.

We had bought some handmade shawls and silver trinkets as souvenirs for Dad and Richard. Mom arranged to have some things shipped, like a new braided rug for the house and a mat for Sam.

She took charge of the handmade fishing knife for Richard, and I took charge of the carved onyx horse for Dad.

We wore some of the jewelry we had bought for ourselves.

"Mom, tell me about Grandma and Grandpa," I asked, sipping the Coke I had ordered.

"Well, they met at Machu Picchu. Your grandfather was here on business; your grandmother was a university student. She was studying archaeology and geography. They fell in love with the rain forest, and each other. That's why your grandmother's portrait shows her holding an orchid. More than ninety species grow here."

"What kind of business was Grandpa on?"

"Well, Peru is one of the largest producers and exporters of copper in the world. They also export several other ores as well as anchovies, fish food and handmade crafts. Grandpa was here to negotiate shipping rights, and he also kept his eyes open for the Agency."

I felt a sudden chill, as if someone was watching us.

"Let's go, Mom," I said.

"What's wrong, Rose? Are you okay?"

"I'm okay, but I think someone is listening to us."

I looked around the other tables, but saw no one suspicious. Mom looked worried now.

Disoriented, we clumsily stood up and gathered our possessions. As we turned to leave an elderly man stood in front of us.

"Excuse me, ladies," he said. "I could not help but overhear. Did you say her grandparents met at Machu Picchu?"

"I don't mean to be rude, sir, but we were not talking to you," Mom replied.

"Forgive me; it is none of my business. But I knew your father. You remind me of him."

"My father is dead. Please excuse us."

But the man would not let us pass.

"Why have you come to Peru?" He asked.

"Again, sir, that is none of your business. Now, must I call the police?"

"No, of course not. I must be mistaken. Forgive my intrusion on your day."

My heart was racing as we left.

"Who was he Mom? Why are we walking so fast?"

"Lots of people knew my father. Some were friends, and some were not. He didn't call him by name. My dad, your grandfather, said all of his friends called him by name."

We were walking faster now. And someone was following. As our footsteps picked up speed, so did his. The old man must have motioned to someone to follow us.

Mom and I looked over our shoulders. There was a man chasing us! He was getting closer, and started to reach for Mom's shoulder…

There was a crash behind us, and people were yelling. We turned to see the man struggling with a vendor, and Paolo getting to his feet. He had tripped the man who went crashing into a vegetable cart.

"Follow me." He said, racing across the street to another shop.

We ran behind him into the little store featuring handmade shawls and lace needlework.

"Grandma, hide us!" Paolo said, parting the curtains and stopping in the small room behind the counter.

The old woman did not question him as we followed.

Mom took out her cell phone as the woman reached for a wooden bat under her counter. She looked like she knew how to use it, too!

"Zip, Code One," Mom said.

Paolo stared at the phone and us. "Who is Zip?" He asked.

"A friend," I said.

"Like me, eh?" Paolo smiled.

"Yes, like you, Paolo," I said.

Within minutes the Peru Travel Service appeared, and so did Dad.

Code one meant 'agent in trouble'. Any available agents would hone in on the signal and come to their aid.

"Dad! Are we glad to see you!"

Paolo introduced his grandmother, Rosa. "Just like my name!" I said, introducing myself.

The three of us told the story as Rosa listened and smiled. She stood with the bat, ready for action.

Rico and Gloria had gone to check the area.

"They are gone," he said when they returned.

"Who were they? Who was the old man?" Mom asked.

"The old man is a member of the Shining Path. His name is Luis Alejandro." Rico explained. "He knew your father had ties to the Agency. Your father was responsible for his arrest many years ago. We don't know who the other man was, he ran away too quickly. But you are not hurt?"

"No, we are not hurt. Thanks to Paolo and his grand-mother," Mom said.

"We are grateful, Senora," Dad said

"My grandson is quick thinking. Do you think we will be safe from these men?" she asked.

"We don't believe they know why we are here. Luis must have recognized me from knowing my father. But since he is still active, we will have to be careful," Mom said.

"We don't think they saw Paolo or where you ran," Gloria said. "They were too busy trying to not make a scene on the street."

"Why are you here?" Rosa asked.

"We're on vacation!" We all said at once.

"Excitement in travel is our slogan!" Rico said.

"Well, it is a pleasure to meet you all. Rose, you must come for lunch at our house while you are here. Paolo has so few friends, and I would like to get to know you better. We have the same names, you know!" Rosa smiled.

Paolo blushed. "But Grandma, they are on vacation and we are poor."

Rosa bristled. "We are not rich in money, true, but your father is a proud fisherman, and works hard to take care of us. Are your friends too good for honest folks?"

"No, of course not, Rosa. Let us check with our friends, and if it is safe for all of us, Rose is welcome to visit. We would not want to endanger your family." Mom said smiling at the old woman.

"No one has asked me if I want to go," I said.

"Well, do you?" Paolo asked hopefully.

"Only if it's okay with my folks," I said, casting puppy eyes at Mom and Dad.

"We can drive her, and cruise the area," Rico said.

"I don't know…" Dad said.

"You'll have to face it sometime, Dad. You can't keep me in a cage forever."

Mom stayed silent. She knew what it was like to be a young girl. She felt for our situation and wished again we were *normal*.

"Well, you'll have to decide soon. There is not enough room in here for all of us, and I have a business to run." Paolo's grandmother snorted.

Rosa parted the curtain and motioned us out of the little room. Mom and I stopped and looked at some of Rosa's work. Dad walked out with Rico and Gloria. I watched as they stood on the street by the car, talking.

Finally Dad came back in. He looked at Paolo, then Rosa, then Mom and me.

"What time would you like Rose to be there?"

Chapter Eight

I was shocked. After what had just happened I thought my parents would never let me out of their sight.

In a way, I was right. I didn't know then that Dad had talked to Rico and Gloria about things other than transportation. Mom didn't either, and kept throwing questioning looks at Dad while they talked to Rosa.

Paolo just looked at me and shrugged. I shrugged back.

"Come on, Rose. Time to go 'till tomorrow at noon. Thank you for your help," Dad said to Paolo and Rosa as we left the shop. He waved at Gloria and Rico, who waved back and drove away.

Back on the Plaza we followed Dad to one of the sidewalk tables and sat down.

"Okay Dad, what's going on?" I demanded.

"Yes, '*Dad*' what's going on?" Mom echoed.

"Well, Rose, honey, you need some time off on this vacation. We need to make sure you'll be okay. Rico and Gloria know Paolo's family, and they assured me they are safe. They will also provide transportation and keep an eye on the area in case you have unexpected company. We can't keep you in a cage forever. Besides, we need to know if we are being watched."

"Oh, I get it, I'm the bait."

"Dear – you can't be serious." Mom said.

"Rose will not be in danger – just chaperoned. We all know why we are here. What we don't know is whether they know why we are here. Our cover is being on a family vacation. We have to mix business with pleasure. Rose, you yourself told us we have to go through with this mission; remember?"

"Yes, Dad, I remember. It's okay, Mom. If we are going to be in a family business as spies, we'll have to get used to it. We all live in a world of cameras anyway."

Mom sighed. "Yes, we do. I lived with security and body-guards as I was growing up, I guess you will, too."

"At least it's not the paparazzi," I said.

"Rose, you know I would never put you in harm's way," Dad said, his eyes showing his fear.

"I know, Dad. I want to visit Paolo and his family. It will be good for my education, and the newsletter. I like to make new friends. The only question I have is do I have to wear the COM link?"

"'Fraid so, kiddo," Dad said with a smile. I knew he was worried about me being with a boy.

"Great, no privacy," I grumbled.

"Don't worry, Rose," Mom said with a knowing smile. "Dad will be tuned out. I'll be listening on the COM. Susan and Steven only get tracking anyway."

I could handle Mom listening. Dad was another matter.

"While we are outside, dear, what did you find out today?" Mom said to Dad.

"The Minister of Commerce promised to arrange a meet-ing between me and Peru Wire. There are two companies here battling for our business, and only one is contracted to work with the Peruvian government. Both companies make everything from fine electrical wire to chain link fencing. One goes after government jobs, supplying fencing to the army; the other works the private sector, going after world markets. The companies are feuding over the right to secure contracts with the U.S.

Our company does not supply the military here. The U.S. feels it would be a conflict of interest should tension develop between the two countries. I told them I was a businessman here with my family on vacation, and looking for a supplier for my company back home."

"Sheesh. And you call me a rambler." I said.

"So far, that's all the information I have."

"We need more details. Can we get copies of the contract from the Agency?" Mom asked.

"No, they are classified, and we no longer have clearance to those documents. What we need to know is why the company is dragging its feet. Why are they stalling? Its not lack of raw material. Peru is the world's second largest producer of copper. I suspect they are trying to delay the new computers the Agency has ordered. They don't want them upgrading, at least not yet," Dad took a breath.

"Makes sense," Mom nodded. "But why?"

"Timing is everything." Dad said. "Could be the stock market. Could be world events or trade talks. Could be they want to use their contract with the U.S. to line up other countries? Maybe their 'war' with the other wire company is slowing them down."

"I'll use the laptop, and do some digging tonight," Mom said.

"Good. I'll send a report to the Agency and update Susan and Steven," Dad said.

"What can I do, Dad?"

"You can show me what you bought today." He said in a teasing voice…

"What makes you think we bought anything today?" I winked at mom.

"The large bulge in your backpack, for one."

"Well, we might have picked up a few things, but I couldn't find anything for you," I fibbed.

Mom looked at me with a questioning expression on her face. Dad hung his head in mock shame and I looked at Mom and went, "Shhh!"

We told him all about our sightseeing, and showed him everything but the horse; I was saving that for later.

"Hey, what about dinner?" Dad said.

"Yes, dear, what *about* dinner? I'm on vacation!" Mom teased.

"Just so happens we have a restaurant back home," he said, referring to the hotel.

"Is that the best you can do? Where is your imagination?" Mom countered.

Dad looked across the street for inspiration. He found it.

"How about McDonald's?" Dad smiled at mom.

Mom groaned, and Dad looked at me for support.

"You're not putting me in the middle on this one, Dad," I said.

"What's wrong with where we are? We are outside a café," he said.

"Yes, we are. But where are the waiters?" Mom asked.

"Let's go in and find out," Dad said, standing up.

We followed him inside. Walking up to the counter, he asked about service.

"Our waiter was injured this afternoon in a fall. You are welcome to eat inside," the man behind the counter replied.

"No thanks." Dad said, knowing what had happened earlier.

We walked across the street to the McDonald's where dad called Rico and Gloria. They would track the waiter and report back.

I smiled as I bit into the Big Mac.

That night after writing my newsletter notes, I said my prayers and my good night's to the three S's-Susan, Steven, and Sam.

I switched off the light and thought about lunch with Rosa and Paolo tomorrow. I thought about Grandma and Grandpa, and the rain forest. I knew there were lots of butterflies there.

I didn't know why, but some of those butterflies must have gotten into my stomach.

Chapter
Nine

This time I was the one who woke everybody up for breakfast. I was excited about going to Paolo's for lunch.

"Come on, sleepy heads! Breakfast is at seven!" I said as I shook Mom and Dad awake at six in the morning.

"Sheesh! Some vacation!" Dad grumbled as he dug further into his pillow.

"We're coming, we're coming." Mom repeated as she sat up against the headboard.

"What a turn around! Some secret agents you are!" I teased.

"Okay, Rose, you scoot, and we'll get up," Dad said.

"Okay, but if you are not ready by seven, I'm leaving without you." It was so much fun to be on the waking up crew for a change.

I went back into the living room, smiling. Sure, it was only a few hours, but I had something to do. I wasn't just a tag along. I knew I'd be watched and listened to, but that did not matter. I wasn't interested in doing anything wrong with Paolo anyway.

While I was waiting for my parents, I made preparations for the day. I unloaded my backpack, and took one of Mom's canvas bags. It would be easier to deal with. I packed my digital camera and notebook. I was a reporter, after all. I decided to wear a pair of shorts, sandals and a t-shirt, since Paolo and his family lived near the coast. And a light nylon windbreaker seemed like a good idea. Maybe we could go out in his Dad's fishing boat. At the last minute I decided to bring my CD player as well.

By the time Mom and Dad came out of their room, I was ready to go.

"Well, too bad we couldn't get you going like this on school days." Mom said.

"I wonder what Rose could be so excited about?" Dad said to Mom, as if I wasn't there.

"Hmm, I wonder…" Mom replied. "Couldn't be a boy, could it?"

"Naw. Must be the job. I think we have a first-class employee on our hands," Dad said, winking at Mom.

I blushed, partly out of embarrassment, and partly out of anger. How dare they tease me about boys.

"Okay, you two. You paid me back. Can't a person just be hungry?" I said, defensively.

"Of course. She's just hungry, dear," Mom said.

"Come to think of it, so am I," Dad said back.

"Let's go eat while we're still friends." I smiled through my teeth.

"Okay, Rose. I'm sorry we teased you. We are hungry. Let's go see what's for breakfast."

And with that, Dad opened the door, and we headed for the hotel dining room.

The restaurant looked different in the daytime. There was a large buffet set up, and the great thing about it was I got to pick whatever I wanted. When we had all loaded our plates, we sat down at one of the window tables.

"By the way, Dad," I said, digging into my scrambled eggs, "did Richard get to the airport on time for his fishing trip?"

"Uhh, yep, got him there okay. He's probably on the Amazon right now."

Something about Dad's answer did not sound right. I decided that Dad must have a good reason for not telling us everything. Maybe it wasn't safe to talk in the dining room, although there were not many people here so early. The buffet ran until eleven. I decided to ask him later.

"Mom, when do we get to go to Machu Picchu?" I asked.

"As soon as we find what we are looking for. In the meantime, there are a couple of museums we could check out."

"You said you were going to tell me about how Grandma and Grandpa met," I reminded her.

"Yes, I know, but after yesterday's events we have to push up the program. We can reschedule."

"Okay, but before the trip is over," I said.

"We've got some calls to make after breakfast, then you and I will get ready for this afternoon," Mom said, business-like.

"Rico and Gloria will pick us up at eleven," Dad said.

"Why so early? Paolo does not live that far way," I asked.

"They are going to drop your mom and me off before they take you there," Dad said quietly.

"I'm already packed. What can I do while we are waiting?" I sure did not want to twiddle my thumbs all morning.

"Well, you could start on your next issue of the newsletter," Mom suggested.

"Good idea. I could write about the Plaza and the places we saw yesterday." I already knew there were things I could not write about.

So after breakfast I took out my laptop, and went to the website. Having been the editor of my school paper was good training for writing a newsletter. In fact, many of the things I learned at school would probably come in handy. Like the first time we ate in the dining room, I knew which fork to use.

Before I knew it, it was ten o'clock and it was time for me to get ready.

"Okay, Rose. Let's check your COM link," Dad said, tapping the barrette in my ponytail.

Mom had her earphone in place. "Got it," she nodded.

"Now I want you to remember Rose, we are not spying on you and Paolo. We're just watching over you in case we run into uninvited guests. Susan and Steven will be tracking your signal through Zip and so will we."

"I know, Dad. I've had some experience in the field, you know." I appreciated what they were doing. They could have held my hand the whole trip, and not let me do anything – and who would have blamed them?

I gave them both a hug and picked up my bag, double-checking the contents like a good agent would.

There was a knock at the door. Mom looked through the peephole.

Our escorts had arrived. And so had the butterflies. I was nervous and excited at the same time. This was going to be some day.

Chapter Ten

The butterflies got worse on the way to Paolo's house. Rico and Gloria made small talk as we rode along in the converted cab. I sat alone in the back seat, slipping from side to side on the hard fake leather upholstery. I hardly heard a word they said.

Mom and Dad had waited a few minutes before leaving the hotel room. They were following in the rental car, but taking a different route. I knew Mom was listening in. She was probably tiring of Rico's chatter. I had tuned everything out.

I was trying not to think about the fact back home Aunt Susan and Uncle Steven were following my 'blip' on Zip, and my parents were chaperoning my first 'date'. If that weren't enough, Rico and Gloria would be watching from a distance.

Sheesh. I felt like the president's daughter. Oh, and let's not forget the possibility several bad guys were probably watching too.

This was too intense. I had to do something to get a little privacy. So, as the car pulled up to the little house on the coast, I finalized my plan.

"Thanks for the ride," I said as I climbed out of the cab, canvas bag slung over my shoulder.

"See you at three," Rico said as they drove away.

By now, Mom and Dad were in position, parked on a scenic overlook, binoculars in hand. Rico and Gloria were headed to another lookout spot. For further security neither location was mentioned. This would also keep me from giving the whole thing away by staring or glaring at my spies.

Knowing Mom was listening, I let Rosa come out and greet me as I walked to the door. As soon as lunch was over I would switch the COM link to tracking only.

"I am so happy you could come, Rose!" Rosa said as we crossed the little yard in front of the little house.

"Thank you for inviting me, Rosa. It's so nice to get away from my parents for a little while. I love them, but sometimes they worry about me too much. It seems like they watch my every move." I knew Mom was wincing at that one.

"Now, Rose, I was young once like you – and I was a parent too. Some day you will thank them for watching over you. But today, I am young like you," She winked at me, and turned away from the door.

"What do you think of my flowers?" She asked.

"They are beautiful, Rosa!" I said, looking at the bright red roses growing in front of the house on either side of the door. They looked even redder against the sea shell pink stucco.

"My husband, rest his soul, and I planted these when we built this little house. This was a shantytown, you know. We started with a few boards and bricks, and built one room. My husband was a fisherman, and I set up a shop for my needlework, and crafts in the Plaza. As time went on we had a son and added another room. As we grew, the house did too. The town grew also, and stretches along the coast."

I looked up and down the street of similar houses. I saw the pride of hard-working people, and realized what a different life I had. Yet my parents worked hard, as did their parents before them. Still, I was lucky to live in the United States.

"Well, lunch is ready, and I know Paolo is waiting to see you," Rosa said, opening the door.

I stepped into the living room of the house. The walls were plastered, and painted bright white. Brightly colored mats hung here and there, hand-made by Rosa. There were also photographs and hand-carved figures of wood done by Paolo's father. It was warm and inviting.

There was a small table in the kitchen at the back of the house. The table was set with hand made placemats and colorful dishes. I could smell the tortillas and chili.

"Where is Paolo?" I asked.

"He was here a moment ago. I asked him to set the table," Rosa said.

The back door opened, and Paolo walked in holding a rose.

"For our guest," he said, handing it to me.

"Thank you," I said, blushing as I took the flower.

"Let me put it in some water," Rosa said. "Sit down and eat, children."

"Paolo, did you pick one of your grandmother's roses for me?" I asked, concerned about him being in trouble.

"No, I have some of my own in back of the house," he smiled.

"Paolo has many talents," Rosa said as she returned with the rose, and set it on the table, "like his father and grandfather."

Tradition was strong in this family. I realized we were more alike than different.

As we ate, my nervousness faded. I forgot about myself and let the reporter in me take over. I learned about Paolo's family and Rosa's business.

"Where is your mother, Paolo?" I asked.

"She died when I was born. My father says I look like her but I think I look like him."

I looked at Paolo's dark hair and eyes. I hadn't seen his mother or father yet.

"Her picture is in the living room, next to Paolo's grandfather," Rosa said. "He died on the fishing boat. His heart gave out pulling in a net of fish. Biggest catch they ever had, his brother said."

"I'm sorry. I guess I'm lucky to have both my parents."

"Rosa is like my mother. She raised me. I am lucky to have my grandmother." Paolo said. "Do you like your grandparents, Rose?"

"They are all gone. But my grandpa and grandma on my mother's side met right here in Peru. At Machu Picchu. My mother is going to take me there, and tell me the story."

"After lunch I will show you the pictures. Father should be home soon, and he has promised to take us for a boat ride." Paolo was excited.

The food was great, and soon we were in the living room of the little house. There on a shelf was a little shrine with photographs of Paolo's mother and grandfather.

"She was beautiful." I said, looking at her dark black hair and dark brown eyes. "What was her name?"

"Luisa. And my grandfather's name was Juan."

I turned at the sound of the new voice. Paolo's father had come home.

"And you are…?" he asked.

"Father, this is Rose, the girl I told you about," Paolo introduced me.

"A pleasure to meet you, Rose. I am Pablo, Paolo's father," he bowed.

"It is nice to meet you, sir," I replied, impressed with the charm of their manners.

Rosa beamed with pride at the family. "Come, Pablo, have some lunch," she said.

"Father, did you remember the boat ride?" Paolo asked.

"Yes, Paolo. You and Rose visit while I eat, and we will take a ride after," Pablo smiled.

I liked his dark, rugged face, and sad, smiling eyes. His hands were weathered and hard working. I looked at his carvings of driftwood.

There were seagulls, a fishing boat; a rose, and an unfinished bust of a woman.

"I started carving after Luisa died. I have never been able to finish her likeness," Pablo said as he walked to the table.

Paolo tugged at me. "Let's wait outside on the beach."

I grabbed the canvas bag, and followed him out the back door.

Paolo showed me his rose bushes. "They are beautiful, Paolo. Is there anything you can't do?"

"Not according to Grandmother. She says I can do anything if I try hard enough."

We went for a walk along the beach. I pointed to a funny looking bird.

"What is that?" I asked.

"That's a Booby. The sailors named them that. They live off tropical islands, and along the coast. Father says they are important for their guano."

"What's guano?" I asked.

Paolo laughed. "Uh, it is used for fertilizer. It is important to the farmers. Father says the guano is drying up because of over fishing the anchovies. Peru is one of the largest exporters of anchovies in the world. They are also used to make fish food, of which we are again the largest producer."

"Yes, I read a lot about your country before we came. Is it true there are more than six million people in Lima?" I asked.

"I do not know I never counted them!" Paolo said, laughing again.

We both laughed and sat down on some rocks. I took out my sun hat and CD player.

"Would you like to hear some music?" I asked.

Paolo nodded and took the CD player and headphones. Ignoring the CD, he tuned in the radio.

"We have many radio stations," he said, and tuned in the local teen station.

"If we are going in the boat, I better put on my sun hat," I said, using it as an excuse to switch the COM link in my barrette from voice to tracking only.

Now my parents would have to rely on their binoculars to watch us. At least we could talk in private.

But before we could do any talking, Pablo walked up and waved us to his boat.

Chapter Eleven

Pablo's boat wasn't very big, but it was big enough for a small crew. It was an old boat, but well cared for.

"This boat feeds many families," Paolo said. "It is not like the big commercial boats that work on the coast. My father and his three brothers are independent fishermen who sell their catch to the fisheries. They fish for tuna and anchovies. Sometimes I fish with them. Every man splits the take and my father counts as two. It is his boat."

Pablo smiled from the pilot house as Paolo showed me around the boat. I took notes for my newsletter. I was glad I had listened to my English teacher, Miss Langtree. She taught me the things every reporter must include in their story, the five "W's" (Who, What, Where, When, and Why.) It also gave me an outline for telling the story.

"What are you doing, Rose?" Paolo asked as I jotted down notes.

"Taking notes for my newsletter. I am a reporter," I said.

"You are a reporter? For whom?" He asked.

"For myself right now. Last year I was the editor of my school paper. Now I am home-schooled, and write a newsletter on the Internet. Someday I will win the Pulitzer prize."

"Wow," Paolo said. "You will be famous."

"Maybe. Well, yes I will be," I said.

"Look, Rose, there are the factories. If you are writing about Peru, you must talk about them. Father says they are our future. We compete with the whole world, he says. Only China beats us in tuna catching."

Pablo had slowed the boat, and I listened to the motor chug quietly as the boat eased along the shore. We stayed far enough out to avoid the other boats and ships busy with their work. Paolo pointed out the fisheries, the handicrafts, and other industries Peru was known for.

"And there are the wire factories. The wire is made from copper and aluminum from the mines in the Andes."

Paolo was proud of his knowledge.

"You know a lot about your country," I said, impressed.

"Father says I am the future of Peru. He does not want me to become a poor, drunken fisherman."

"Someday you will be famous too." I said.

Paolo smiled, and stood a little taller.

My mind turned to my parents. I wished I hadn't turned off the COM link. I knew they would be watching, though.

"Paolo, can you show me the wire factories?"

"I just did," Paolo said with a quizzical look.

"No, I mean take me there."

"Sure, but why?" Paolo asked with his brows furrowed.

"Well, it's a long story, but let's just say I want to write about them."

"Okay. I could see you at the hotel tomorrow. I will be working there in the morning. At lunchtime maybe your parents would let me take you," Paolo said with a little excitement in his voice.

"We can't tell them about it," I said. "But maybe they will let you take me to McDonald's. Then we could go to the factories."

Paolo agreed, and we made our plans. I knew my parents would not let me go alone, and I knew if they were there, I would never find out anything. I didn't tell Paolo I wasn't just a reporter; I was a spy, also.

Pablo took us out to the fishing grounds. I took the camera out of my bag, and took pictures of Paolo and his father. I took pictures of the other boats and the scenery. I had been careful not to take pictures around the factories. You never knew who was watching.

Pablo took us back to the house and at exactly three o'clock Rico and Gloria drove up.

I said goodbye to Rosa and Pablo, and walked to the car with Paolo.

"Thank you for the nice tour, Paolo. See you soon," I said as I climbed into the tour car, winking at Paolo.

He nodded at the wink, knowing as kids do, that something was supposed to be a secret. He didn't know why, but went along with it.

"See you soon," he repeated, shutting the door of the converted cab.

I knew I was in for some questions!

I braced myself for the five W's!

Chapter Twelve

"Well, young lady how was your day?" Rico asked as I slid across the slick back seat.

I did not like Rico's tone. Why was it all adults called you 'young lady, or young man' when they were upset with you?

"Well, *Dad*, it was very nice," I replied tartly. Only my parents had the right to call me 'young lady'.

"Your voice link was off, Rose. We were worried about you," Gloria said defensively.

"You weren't supposed to be hearing me," I said.

"No, we weren't. Your mother told us she had lost voice. You didn't do that on purpose, did you?"

"Why, no," I said, "It must have accidentally switched off when I put my sunhat on."

Gloria looked at me, and kind of smiled. It was hard to fool another woman. Especially an agent.

"Well, everything turned out fine. We did not see any threats." Gloria said more to Rico than me.

Rico relaxed, and I launched into a description of the boat ride, conveniently leaving out the wire factories. I bored them with facts about fishing they already knew.

By the time they dropped me at the hotel, they were convinced I was just another twelve-year-old kid, and they were glad the babysitting was over.

Mom and Dad were another matter. They arrived at the same time. Dad dropped Mom at the door and went to park the car. I didn't give Mom a chance to ask anything. I ran up to her with my digital camera to show her the pictures.

"Hi, Mom! Look at these neat pictures! I got to ride in the fishing boat! Look at this one!"

I was so happy and bubbly Mom forgot her questions. She did not want to spoil the good time I had.

By the time we got to the room, and Dad walked in, we were both laughing about boys.

Dad did not have a chance. He walked into the room ready to fire questions, but stopped in his tracks when we both looked at him and started to laugh.

"Hey, what's so funny?" He said.

At that we laughed again. Soon he was laughing too.

"Boys." Mom said, looking at me.

"Yep!" I said, smiling lovingly at Dad, who melted under it.

He started to say something, but stopped and shook his head. He would never figure it out.

"Well, Rose, how was your day?" He finally asked.

"It was great, Dad. Can't wait to show you the pictures!"

There was no way Dad was going to spoil his daughter's joy. After all, here we were safe and sound, laughing and having fun. Everything was fine.

I showed him the pictures on the digital camera, and talked about the newsletter.

"I must admit, Rose, we were a little worried when we lost your voice link. We watched your boat ride through the binoculars. At least your tracking was on," he said.

Rats! I thought I had gotten his mind off that.

"Must have been my sunhat, Dad."

"That's what we figured, too," he said, winking at Mom.

Sheesh! Could a girl ever get any privacy in this world? At least they weren't mad at me.

"You know, Dad, Rosa said she remembered what it was like to be a parent and a kid," I said thoughtfully.

"We do, too," Dad smiled.

"She said I should be glad I have parents who care about me."

"We do, Rose. We care about you having a good time, too. Remember, we are on the same side. So many kids think parents are their enemy. We know you wouldn't get into any bad things."

I felt bad about my secret plan to visit the wire factories, but knew Mom and Dad would never agree with it. I wanted to help them on my own. I decided to not to tell them.

"Hey, where are we going to eat tonight?" I asked, switching tracks.

"Well, we had a busy day. How about right here in our room?" Dad said.

"Okay by me. I can download my pictures onto the website and work on my newsletter."

"Yeah, and we have to coordinate with Susan and Steven," Mom spoke up.

"Can we put them on Zip?" I asked. "I want to see Sam. I miss him."

"Sure can," Mom said.

The best thing a girl can do after a date is spend lots of time with her parents. That way they don't worry about losing their little girl.

We ate in our room, and called home.

"Susan, Steven. Good to see you." Dad said to the hologram on Zip.

It was like having them in our room. I knew we were appearing the same way there. Sam barked at our images, and I reached to pet him. He whined when he didn't feel my hand, and cocked his head from side to side. Finally he lay down, and whimpered a little.

"What have you found out?" Dad asked.

"So far, someone in the Agency is a mole. We are checking records now to see who is tipping off the Peruvians about your presence there. We are sure he or she is part of the plan to delay the shipment of the wire. Your theory about delaying the updated computers to the Agency seems correct. Someone is planning something big, and does not want us to find out before it happens," Steven reported.

"Have you identified the waiter yet?" Mom asked.

"Yes. Pedro Alveraz, known student of the Old Fox of Shining Path. Your father tipped the authorities to his activities in the seventies which led to the arrest of most of the Shining Path members. They know his shipping contacts were only part of his reason for being in Peru. They see your visit there as more than a vacation, and getting information will be very hard for you. They will do nothing to damage relations with the United States again – especially if they are involved in the coming event. They will only stall you, and throw out false information."

"How can we get around it?" Mom asked.

Susan spoke now. "Keep tracking communications through your business computers. Look for any links you can establish or coded messages. Maybe they have been careless here and there. They will not allow you access to their computers physically. You will have to work through Zip, Rico, and Gloria."

"I have a meeting with the wire company tomorrow." Dad said. "At least I will get to look around. I am posing as a businessman, but they know better."

This was news to me. I hoped Dad would not be at the factory the same time I was.

"Keep your COM link on, and your button cam," Steven said. "What time is your tour?"

"Eight a.m. I should be out of there by ten."

Whew! I was planning on being there with Paolo about twelve-thirty.

"Any news on the man on the plane?" Dad asked.

"We've been tracking his movements," Steven replied. "His presence seems to indicate a joint effort in the plan between the hard-line Communists, and the terrorists. Whatever they are planning must be pretty big. So far we have the Al-Qaeda terrorists, Shining Path, and the Communists working together. I wouldn't be surprised to run into the Colombian drug lords too."

"Somebody's computer must have information in it." Mom said. "I'll hook up tonight with my company computers. There must be flags somewhere."

"With all the Agency's resources, why haven't we heard anything?" Susan asked.

"Word of mouth. They must be setting it all up with a code of silence," Dad said.

"We'll keep working from this end," Steven said. "Right now we're going to have some breakfast."

"We just finished supper," Mom said

"Good night, Rose." Susan said as they signed off. Samson the Great barked as I faded out,

"Good night," I said, choking back a tear at Sam's bark.

The rest of the evening was spent working on laptops. I edited my newsletter and Mom searched her company computers for information. Dad read up on wire production and mining.

Finally it was time to get ready for bed. I stood on the balcony looking out at the lights of Lima at night. Everything looked so peaceful. I watched the cars below, and listened to the traffic. I wondered how many people knew something terrible was being planned.

Maybe they just didn't want to think about it.

Chapter Thirteen

But I did think about it. All night long. The excitement I had planning my espionage with Paolo faded with the realization of world events. All my brave talk seemed to click off with the light. I felt like a twelve-year-old child.

Eventually I did drop off to sleep, just before dawn. The light shining through the curtains brought some of my courage back. Stumbling to the bathroom, I gave myself a good talking to.

"Get a hold on it, now," Grandpa used to tell me when I'd fall off my bike. "Get right back up and tame that horse!"

How was I ever going to be a world-class reporter if I couldn't go after a story? I could never look myself in the eye again if I backed out now. I decided to get back on that bike.

I put on jeans, a t-shirt, and my Reeboks. I threw my hair into a quick ponytail, and put on my Yankee's ball cap. I packed my canvas bag with a note pad, and my digital camera as I had done the day before. I made sure my barrette was in place, and switched to tracking only.

There was rain forecast for Lima today so a windbreaker would be wise, too.

Finally suited up, and my courage restored, I stepped into the living room of the suite and asked, "What's for breakfast?"

Mom and Dad were both up and sitting on the couch. They had been talking quietly so as not to wake me. They were surprised to see me.

"Well, good morning, Rose. My, you are up and at 'em today." Mom said, setting down her coffee cup.

"Going to the ball game?" Dad asked.

"No, the T.V. said rain today, that's all," I replied matter-of-factly.

"Well, we both have to work today," Dad said. "Let's catch the breakfast buffet and we'll talk about our plans."

"How late were you going to let me sleep?" I asked

"Just until you woke up," Mom said. "I'll be here all day, and I thought you might hang out with me while I work."

"That sounds exciting", I said flatly.

I was trying to find some way to have lunch with Paolo so we could get away long enough to check out the wire factory.

"Well, let's eat. I'm hungry," I said, turning toward the door.

Mom and Dad looked at each other and shrugged. They figured I was just cranky, and not excited about sitting there all day, especially when we were supposed to go to Machu Picchu today.

Ah. There was my leverage. I would pretend to be so disappointed about our change in plans that Mom would have to let me go with Paolo. I smiled as we trudged down the hall to the elevators.

Nobody talked in the elevator. I think it's a law or something. I used the silence to maximum advantage. I wanted my parents to feel guilty about having to work.

By the time we got to the dining room, I knew I had them.

"My, you sure are hungry, Rose." Mom said as we sat down.

"People eat more when they travel, I heard," I replied, setting down a heaping plate of scrambled eggs and fruit. "Isn't that right, Dad?" It was still good strategy to play one parent against the other.

"So I've heard," he said, straddling his chair as he set down his plate.

"What time are you leaving, Dad?" I asked.

"Right after breakfast, sweetheart. I have to be at the wire factory at eight."

I put on a sad face, but did not want to over-do it. I did not want him to cancel his tour on my account.

"Look," Mom said, "isn't that Paolo?"

There was Paolo, dressed in his hotel whites, at the buffet. He was loading a big plate also.

Looking up, he noticed us and waved

Dad waved him over. "Come and sit with us, Paolo," he said.

"Dad, don't do that." I scolded.

But it was too late. Paolo came to our table, and sat next to me.

"I get a free breakfast when I work at the hotel," he informed us.

"Well, we wanted to thank you for showing Rose your father's boat yesterday. "

"She had such a good time," Mom piped up.

71

"Yes, thank your grandmother for us, also," Dad said.

I wondered why Paolo was not dressed like me, and then realized how smart that was. This way no one would suspect we were planning anything. I figured he would work until noon, and then change into his street clothes.

"Well, you kids are sure eating well this morning," Mom said again. Paolo and I had laid out our plans yesterday on the boat. We would both dress in jeans and windbreakers, and eat a big breakfast. I would find some way to get Mom to let me eat lunch at McDonald's alone and instead I would meet Paolo and we would run down to the wire factory and look around. We wanted to disguise ourselves as a couple of American kids just looking around. We could gather information to help the investigation and at the same time I could show my parents I could help too. After all, I was twelve years old!

"Well, I have to get to work," Dad said, pushing his chair back. "You kids have a nice day."

"You, too, Dad," I said, kissing him on his cheek as he bent down, embarrassing Paolo a great deal!

"Yes, dear, you be careful out there!" Mom said as he kissed her.

"I must get to work, also," Paolo said as he stood up, holding his empty plate.

"I hope you don't expect a kiss," I teased.

Blushing, he looked at Dad. "Yech. Why would I want that?"

Now my face was red.

Dad laughed and walked away. Mom was holding back a laugh also.

"Serves you right for teasing Paolo like that," she said.

I kept my smile to myself.

Chapter Fourteen

My plan was working perfectly.

I started on Mom as soon as we left the breakfast table. I knew guilt would be my only weapon in getting her to let me go with Paolo.

"Aw, Mom, do you have to work today? I thought we could go to Machu Picchu or something."

"Now Rose, you know how important this is. Why don't you work on your newsletter? Besides, it's supposed to rain anyway."

I could hear the guilt in Mom's voice. Perfect.

Turning the key to our suite, Mom opened the door and let out a sigh. She wasn't excited about working either. I only hoped she wouldn't change her mind. I had to be careful not to lay it on too thick.

It was nine-thirty. Both of us had been slaving away at our laptops for a whole hour. I let out a "Ho-Hum" followed by a soft sigh just loud enough for Mom to hear it. Her ears cocked in my direction just like Sam's always did. She did not turn her head.

We kept working in heavy silence.

Paolo got off duty at noon. He changed into his jeans and sneakers, and stepped into the elevator, ready for part two of our plan.

By now, Dad should be finished with his tour of the wire factory. We had to hurry so we would not cross paths.

Paolo knocked lightly at our door.

"Well, Paolo. How nice to see you! Please come in," Mom said. "Are you finished working today?"

"Well, sort of," he replied. "I have to go into the plaza to pick up some supplies for the hotel. I could use some help. Could Rose come along?"

"Oh, I don't know, Paolo. Rose should stay here until her father returns."

"Oh, can I, Mom? We have been working for hours. I'm so bored! Please," I pleaded.

"But it may not be safe, Dear," Mom defended her position.

"I'll wear my COM," I said, anxious to reassure her.

"She will be safe with me," Paolo said, standing tall and throwing his shoulders back.

It was so cute Mom was thrown off guard.

"Well…" she said.

I knew she was starting to crack.

"It's only for an hour or so," Paolo said.

"Really, Mom. We'll be okay,"

"Oh, I hope your father doesn't find out."

"Gee, thanks Mom!" I jumped ahead.

"Wait a minute; I didn't say it would be okay."

"But you were going to, weren't you?" I said, with big innocent eyes no parent can resist.

"If your Dad finds out…" Mom threatened.

"I'll get my windbreaker!" I said, grabbing the bag I had already prepared.

"Let's go! Thanks Mom, you're the greatest!" I shouted as we rushed out the door.

"Be back in an hour…" she shouted down the hall as we vanished into the elevator.

The silent whoosh of the closing doors signaled our escape. I looked at Paolo and smiled.

"Nice work, partner." I said, shaking his hand.

"Nice work, partner," he repeated.

"Let's get out of here before Dad comes back. I hope you know the way, Paolo."

"Of course I do. This is my town," he said, smiling.

By the time we heard the "ding" of the first floor elevator we had synchronized our watches and finalized our plan.

The spies at the wire factory would be no matches for us.

Chapter Fifteen

Paolo turned right as the doors opened. We were going out the back. On the way he picked up his windbreaker. No one paid attention as we went out the back door of the hotel. They were used to Paolo coming and going.

The sky was dark and cloudy, and there was a light rain falling. This was unusual for Lima, and most people welcomed the rain. The air smelled fresher, and the streets were wet and shiny.

Paolo knew all of the back streets, and soon we were not far from the coast highway. It was too far to walk to the factory, but Paolo said we were going to meet his uncle.

His uncle was a truck driver. He owned a van, and picked up shipments at the airport. He delivered them to the factories along the coast.

"Paolo, you are one minute late!" Paolo's uncle looked at both of us with a scowl on his face.

"Sorry, Enrico. Rose, this is my uncle, Enrico."

"Nice to meet you, Enrico," I said, climbing into the van behind Paolo.

Enrico ground the gears and the van lurched forward. I grabbed the handle of the side door, and hung on as the van picked up speed. We lurched through every gear until at last we were rolling along the coast highway.

"So, you are a reporter, eh?" Enrico said. "They start young in your country, eh?"

"Some day I will win the Pulitzer Prize." I said, smiling under my Yankee's hat.

"Paolo tells me you only need a little time to take some pictures. Will you take one of me? Maybe you will write about my delivery service, yes?"

"I'll take one when we jump out," I said.

"Well, here we are. I will be back in half an hour. I have deliveries to make. You must be here, or find your own ride."

"We will, Uncle," Paolo assured him.

"Smile." I said as I snapped the camera.

"What kind of camera is that? It does not look like other cameras. Do you have enough film?" Enrico asked.

"It's digital. It doesn't need film," I explained.

Enrico smiled as I took the picture, seemingly unconcerned about our mission.

"Half an hour." He reminded us as he drove away.

Paolo and I stood in the rain looking at the chain link fence of the Peru Wire Company.

"Don't get too close, Rose," he cautioned.

I started snapping pictures of the giant wooden spools of wire and cable behind the fence.

It was just like I remembered from Grandpa's story. There were spools of different colored wire. Each of the giant spools sat in a big open area, and there was a forklift moving them around, probably to make room for more.

I wished we could have gone on the tour with Dad to see how the wire was made. I had read about how wire was made on Zip.

The copper or aluminum was made into rods, and forced through diamond cutters that shaved them down to the thickness desired. The blades had to be made of something very hard so as not to wear out.

I had also read about the growing wire business in Peru and how the two wire companies were at war with each other for business. Curiously, wire imports to the U.S. from Peru had doubled six months before the last election.

"Rose, you are getting too close!" Paolo whispered as I continued snapping pictures.

"I need to get the lens through the fence," I explained. "Keep watch for me."

Paolo was getting nervous. He did not like the camera so close to the building, where they could be seen.

"Rose…" he started to say.

"Shhh." I said as I heard voices from the wire yard.

We both stood silently, listening.

"I tell you, I don't trust that American businessman."

"Of course we know he is a spy. He is here to investigate the delay in the shipment of wire to the U.S."

The voices were coming from between two spools of wire. I motioned Paolo to be quiet, and moved a few steps to the right. Now I had a better view. The men were dressed in business suits, and one of them looked familiar.

It was the old man from the Plaza. The Shining Path member my grandfather had put away years before.

Paolo recognized him also, and tugged at my sleeve. I squatted down low as the two men continued talking.

"This plan has taken years to put together, all by word of mouth. The few things the Americans can find on their computers will not be enough to stop it unless they succeed in their plan to upgrade their computers, and link them all into one network. Our part of the plan is just to stall the wire. We must not draw undue attention to ourselves. We will not interfere with the American or his family. As president of this wire factory, I am taking all the risks, delaying our delivery."

Now I recognized the other man. Alex Bacon, the man on the plane.

"I say we stop the Americans now." The Old Fox said. "They can find out too much. We can make them vanish. This is the largest combined terrorist effort ever conceived. All of the anti-U.S. forces are involved. We cannot risk the plan."

"Our orders are just to delay and confuse. We will stick to the plan. By the time the Americans get their wire, all three bridges will be destroyed, and their economy will be in ruins."

Paolo was crouched low, and backing up. There was a growing look of terror on his face. This was a bigger story than he wanted to know. My heart was pounding as I snapped a picture of the two men.

"Which three bridges?" I whispered.

"The Brooklyn Bridge, The Golden Gate and the…" the Old Fox said almost as if he had heard me, but before he could finish his sentence I fell backwards into Paolo's lap. He fell backwards into the street, and the horn of a passing car caused the men to look right at us.

We scrambled to get to our feet, slipping on the wet pavement. The camera went sliding along the curb as we grabbed each other's windbreakers, and tried to stand up.

By the time we did, it was too late! Standing behind us the two men clasped each of our necks with their big hands.

The Old Fox took the Yankee's cap from my head and spun me around.

"The girl from the Plaza! The American's daughter, and my old nemesis' granddaughter."

I wished I had turned on the COM link. I hoped he wouldn't see it.

They searched our jackets and my bag.

"What are you doing here, children?" one of them asked.

"What did you hear?" the other asked.

"Nothing. She is a tourist. I was giving her a tour," Paolo said, bravely.

"I just wanted to see a factory," I said.

"What should we do with them?" the president asked.

"I know what I would like to do with them." the Old Fox replied.

Both of us were scared now.

"We will make them disappear!"

"You mean kill them?"

"We could, but it would bring too much attention. I know there is a wire on the girl. She must be spying for her father. Ah, I think I know…"

He was looking at my hair. He had found the COM link. If only I had set it to voice we would be rescued soon. But it was set on tracking only.

"Come with us, children," he said, as he removed the barrette from my hair, and replaced my cap.

Paolo struggled, and I kicked, but it did no good. They dragged us through the gate into the wire yard. Just before we got to the garage door, the Old Fox stopped.

"Hold them!" He said, taking the COM link and slowly inching his way towards a booby bird perched on one of the spools.

"Oh no." I whispered as I saw what he was about to do.

Many of the boobies were tame, and he reached into his pocket as if to take out some food.

The bird fell for the deception, and with one quick move, the Old Fox grabbed it, and fastened the COM link to its leg. Then he threw the bird into the air, yelling and terrorizing it so it would not return.

Our hope of rescue was headed for parts unknown.

"So, you want to see a factory, eh? Well, now you will have a personal tour!"

As we were dragged inside, I looked at Paolo. I knew he was thinking the same thing. They didn't know about Enrico, and the camera lying in the street.

At least we had some hope of rescue.

Chapter
Sixteen

"Smile, children, or else!" the Old Fox said, as we walked through the garage door, hands still clutching our necks. We smiled at the forklift driver, and he smiled back. The workers rolling big wooden spools of wire from here to there all smiled as we walked by, apparently delighted to see two smiling young children in their dreary world.

No one seemed to think anything unusual was happening. They smiled for their boss, too, who seemed to be steering us away from the factory and toward the offices. We stopped at an office.

Still clutching Paolo's neck, the man from the plane opened a door with a different name on it: Alexis Bogdonovich, President and C.E.O. of the Peru Wire Company. *Aha. Things were beginning to make sense now.*

"What are we going to do with them?" the Old Fox asked.

"Patience, Bernard. I have an idea."

"Bernard?" I asked. "Your name is Bernard? No wonder you call yourself the Old Fox." My anger popped up in sarcasm.

"Quiet, feisty one, or I'll solve the problem right here. I do not call myself the Old Fox. It is a sign of respect from the members of The Shining Path."

"Oh, I get it, they would laugh at Bernard!" I just couldn't keep quiet.

"We will take the children on a real tour, and then we will show them where the copper comes from – or used to come from –" Alexis said.

I wondered if he knew Vladimir, but then realized his other identity was the president of Porcel-Art, the supplier of cheap mass-produced phony Russian porcelain Vladimir sold to discount stores across the USA to raise money for the Communist hard-liners; he definately knew Vladimir. I remembered Dad saying how the terrorists needed financing, and camouflage to operate.

"Yes, that is a good idea," Bernard said, nodding. "No one would suspect anything."

Paolo was quiet through the whole conversation. I knew he was scared, and so was I, but he was looking for a way to escape.

The door opened, and again the big hands were placed on our necks as we were steered out of the office and back into the factory.

We were led past big steaming cauldrons where the copper was separated from the ore, then past the cooling bins, and finally the molds where the hot liquid copper and aluminum were made into rods.

Then we were hustled by the cutters where the rods were forced through diamond jigs where they were reduced to various sizes of wire. We watched the process with little explanation from our tour guides.

Along the way some workers smiled at us, and others looked annoyed. Alexis stopped a man and said something to him. He smiled and nodded, then left. We wondered what his assignment was until we were led to the roof of the building, and a waiting helicopter.

The chopper was plain white with only call letters on it. It was executive class, though and we instinctively ducked as we were pushed on board.

As soon as we were thrown into our seats the pilot lifted off.

The rain had stopped and the clouds had blown away. Lima was once again the sunny, historic city we had known.

Even though I was used to flying, my heart was pounding. By now, Mom must have figured out we had not gone out for supplies. Dad would be back, and very angry. No, probably scared – worried something had happened to us.

I wished I had never thought of my brilliant plan. I clutched my canvas bag and looked at Paolo. It looked like he had never flown before. I thought about the camera and Paolo's Uncle Enrico, and hoped he would find it. With the COM link gone the way of the booby, it might be our only hope of being found.

I wanted to talk to Paolo about it, but stayed quiet.

As we headed toward the mountains, Bernard spoke up. "We could drop them, you know."

"No. Our part of the plan is only to delay and confuse. We cannot risk killing them. We will leave them in the old mining shack at the top of the mountain. No one has been there during the winter. If they escape, they will have to survive the mountain, and by the time they return – if they return – it will be too late. We cannot risk our contact, and if they are found dead, they could link them to the factory and set off an investigation that could shut down the mission."

"You are just afraid of losing your position and money!" The Old Fox replied. "I have a score to settle with this one," he said, pointing at me.

"Your score was with her grandfather," Alexis said.

I looked out the window at the mountain peaks. They were high, rocky, and covered with snow. The thaw had just begun, and we could feel the cold air. At least we were wearing some kind of jackets!

I hoped they would be enough.

Chapter Seventeen

The nylon windbreakers weren't enough. I could feel the chill already. Paolo was toughing it out, but I could see he was cold, too.

"Where are we?" I demanded to know.

"We are finishing our tour," the Old Fox replied.

"Here is where the wire comes from. This is a copper mine approximately fifteen hundred feet up the mountain. This mine is now played out, and ceased production last fall. Here is the mining shack. This completes our tour. You will now follow us inside the shack for a closer look at the miner's life," Alexis said in a tour guide's voice.

"That's okay," Paolo said, "I am not that curious."

"Oh, but I think you are." the Old Fox tightened his grip on Paolo's neck and pushed him inside.

"You, too, Rosie," he said, reaching for my neck as well.

"Don't call me Rosie. It makes me angry. You wouldn't like it when I get angry."

"Angry is good. It will give you a chance to survive," he said.

"We will survive. We'll get down and tell what we know and then you'll be in big trouble. When my Dad and Uncle Richard get through with you…" I was angry, very angry, and it was evident in my face.

"If you do survive the mountain, it will be too late, and we'll be gone. The world will change, and your father will be powerless to stop it. Remember, we could kill you – but we won't. We are giving you a chance."

"My grandfather stopped you once, and I will stop you again."

"Enough threats, child. Hold still while I tie your hands or it will hurt more," the Old Fox spat out the words.

Before long, Paolo and I were tied up and sitting across from each other on the floor of the old shack. We listened to the helicopter take off, powerless to stop it. Soon we faced the reality of being alone, tied up in an old shack 1,500 feet high in the Andes Mountains.

On top of that, the bad guys were getting away. Three bridges in the USA were about to be destroyed. Thousands of people would die. The whole world economy would suffer. Our parents were worried sick about us. If we could get down from the mountain, they would probably kill us themselves.

I wanted to cry, but I was facing Paolo. I didn't want him to see me. I wanted to be alone but was glad I wasn't. I remembered being kidnapped in Russia. I got through it okay with the help of some new friends. I would get through this okay, too.

Paolo was trying to be brave. The same thoughts must have been running through his head also. He couldn't cry in front of a girl.

"Rose, slide over to me. Let me untie your hands," He said.

I used my feet to inch across the rough floor of the shack. I was glad I had worn jeans. Reaching Paolo, I turned around and let him untie me. Even though his hands were tied also, he was able to use his fingers, and worked at the ropes until at last they fell away.

"Now I'll untie you," I said and went to work on his ropes.

Soon we were both free, and standing in the old shack. We looked around for anything that could help us.

"Have you ever been in the mountains, Paolo?" I asked.

"Not this high. Just the foothills. Have you?"

"Once, at camp in Arizona. But I never really did any climbing. It was a riding camp. My uncle Richard did teach me some survival things, though."

"Well, let's see what we can find to help us. It's a long way down," Paolo said.

I looked around the old shack. There was a coil of rope, an old pickax, and a box of crackers with one unopened sleeve. I hoped they would be edible. My stomach was growling already.

We opened the crackers right away. They were dry, but okay. Water. There was no water! What I would have given for a Coke.

"What will we do for water?" I asked.

"Well, there is a stove and one old pan. We could melt some snow," Paolo said, excited.

"Good idea!" I said, grabbing the old pan.

There were a few unburned logs stacked alongside the stove, and Paolo threw some in and looked for a match.

We were lucky to find some on the ledge of the old, dirty window and while Paolo worked on the fire, I went outside to get the snow.

The wind was blowing, and the afternoon was beginning to fade. I knew it would get colder.

I stopped to look around. The view was amazing! There were mountains in all directions. At this altitude all I could really see were snow covered peaks and clouds.

As I walked around the shack with the pan, I looked down on green plateaus and ledges. Far down to the east I could see the Amazon River and the treetops of the jungle.

I wondered if Richard was enjoying his fishing. By now, he would have been called back to look for us.

As the smoke wound from the little chimney in the shack, I realized how small I really was.

"Needles in a haystack," I said to myself as I carried my thimbleful of snow to the little shack.

"We're just two needles in a haystack," I repeated.

Chapter Eighteen

"Needles in a haystack," Richard said when he got the news. "Two kids lost in Lima – needles in a haystack."

I did not know Richard had not left Lima. He wasn't on a fishing trip. He had gone deep undercover into the nightlife of Lima to find information. He was hanging out at the kind of clubs that kids aren't supposed to know about.

Waking up at five p.m. in a sleazy hotel room, he read the message on the cell phone. It said ZIP.

"The suitcase is open," he said into the phone.

"But the bag is zipped. Richard, Rose is missing!" came my father's frantic voice.

"What? How can that be?" Richard asked, suddenly awake.

"She went with Paolo to pick up supplies for the hotel this afternoon just before I returned from the wire factory. She never returned, and Paolo is missing too."

"What about her COM?" Richard asked.

"She must have set it on tracking only. We are getting a signal, but can't get a fix. It seems to be moving all over Lima. First by car, and then by boat. Doesn't make sense." Dad was trying hard to control his feelings.

"What do you mean?" Richard asked.

"Well, first the signal is on land, and then it seems to be over the water. We have the Lima police, Rico and Gloria tracking the signal, but they haven't got a sighting yet."

"Where was the last permanent fix?"

"Outside the wire factory. Rose must have gone there on her own with Paolo's help. I think she is trying to help us with the case. The police are there now."

"Where are you?" Richard asked.

"I'm here with her mother. She blames herself for letting Rose go. One of us needs to stay here in case they return or we get a call."

"Do you want me to come in?" Richard asked.

"No. Stay undercover and see what you can find out. You might be the one who can get a lead. Susan and Steven have been alerted and all the Agency computers are looking for any communications."

"Okay. I was just getting ready for the night shift. I have a date with a former Shining Path girlfriend. I'm seeing her tonight at the Pizzaro Club."

"Good. Let's hope someone drinks too much and talks too much. We'll send word by Zip as soon as we hear anything."

"Okay. I'll set my phone on vibe, and call you if I get any leads. They better pray they haven't harmed her." Richard said.

"We'll both pray they haven't." Dad said, signing off.

Richard went into the shower.

"Needles in a haystack. You always find them the hard way."

The trouble was they were looking in the wrong haystack.

Chapter Nineteen

We were tired, cold, hungry, and scared. Even though we wanted to start climbing down the mountain, we decided to wait. It would be too hard to see in the dark, too dangerous, and too cold.

We would have to wait until morning. Sitting on the floor of the old shack, we made our plans. First, we divided up the food. One stack of crackers was not going to get us far.

"I wish we had some peanut butter or jelly," I said, hearing my stomach rumble.

"I wish we had anything," Paolo said.

"You need peanut butter to keep the jelly from running through the holes in the crackers," I went on.

"Well, we don't have any jelly so what is the difference?" Paolo asked.

"The difference is it gives me something to think about besides being stuck on top of this mountain." I snapped back.

Paolo winced. "I'm sorry, Rose. I should have never shown you the wire factory. Now everyone will be worried about us."

"I don't know what got in to me. I guess I just wanted to show my parents I could do something on my own."

"We'll be okay, Rose. I am a survivor and from what you have told me, you are too. We're not just two little kids."

"We have to figure out a way to sleep," I reminded him, a little embarrassed.

"And other things, like the bathroom," he blushed.

"That's easy, we just take turns," I said.

"As for sleeping, there is an old rug by the stove. We could shake it out, and you could sleep on it. I will sleep sitting up against the wall," Paolo said.

"Well, the first part is okay, but it will get cold even with a fire. In survival training they told us the best thing to do in the cold was to sleep together to save body heat." Now I was blushing.

"Okay. Let's do our chores before it gets too dark. Then we can sleep, and get up at first light. We have a lot of hiking to do tomorrow," Paolo said, taking charge.

I looked at the old, braided rug. I sure did not want to put my face on it. I decided I could empty my canvas bag and sleep on that.

I stood up and stretched. Grabbing the old rug from the floor I was surprised at how heavy it was. It was not very big, and must have been full of dirt and mud. Years of miners tracking it up. Sheesh.

Paolo helped me drag it outside. We hung it on a rock and beat it with sticks. Clouds of dirt and dust flew in the wind. Finally, it was lighter, and we shook it out. We decided to hang it on a rock for a while to freshen it up.

Paolo went around to the other side of the shack to freshen himself up. I stood looking down the mountain trying to find a path. That's when I saw the smoke.

"Paolo. Come here. Quick." I yelled.

"What is it, Rose?" he asked, running around to my side of the shack.

"Smoke. A chimney. Someone lives on this mountain." I was so excited I was still yelling.

"That's great. That is wonderful." Paolo was yelling, too.

"Let's plan a route." I said.

The smoke was coming from below us and to the west. We had to guess but it looked like it was about a quarter of the way down. It looked like we could reach them in a few hours.

"But not tonight," Paolo said.

We went back inside, and laid out our gear. The rope was about twenty feet long, we guessed. The pick ax, matches, crackers and my canvas bag. Inside my bag were the CD player, headphones, a notebook, a pen, and a water bottle with a cap! The bottle was empty from the day before, but we could fill it up with melted snow. The tin pan could stay behind.

We could make it!

We were too excited to sleep, and too nervous. We stalled as long as we could. We brought in the rug, and took off our shoes. We didn't have a blanket, and would have to find a way to keep our feet warm.

"Why are we taking off our shoes?" Paolo asked.

"Because, our feet will sweat, and be colder in the morning. We have to hike in them," I said.

"But how will we keep them warm tonight?" He asked.

"Well, before we go to sleep we can put them on loosely without tying them. That should be enough to keep them from sweating and still keep warm."

"Okay, that sounds like a good idea," he said.

We each took a cracker to sleep on and a sip of water. There was only one log left, and we put it in the stove. It would have to do.

We talked into the night, and finally gave up. We would have to find a way to sleep. The fire was not warm enough, and the wind howled through the cracks in the old boards. We wouldn't freeze, but it would be close.

I wished I had Sam with me. The big old Newfie sneaked up on my bed many times, and I used to pretend not to notice. I woke up with my arms around him many mornings.

"Paolo, you lie down and face the wall. I'll lay with my back to you."

"Okay," he said, nervously.

"It's a matter of survival," I said, matter-of-factly.

"Yes, you are right. Goodnight," he replied.

As the moon came up through the dirty window, and the glow of the fire flickered on the wall through the door of the stove, I smiled and shook my head.

"Too intense." I thought as my back rubbed up against his. I put my head on the canvas bag, glad that Mom had suggested I bring it on the trip.

"Good for souvenirs and shopping," she had said.

I felt bad for Paolo sleeping on the old, dirty rug. He did not move or say a word.

Soon, I found it more comfortable to turn the other way, and I threw my arm around him, cuddling up as if he were Sam. I felt him stiffen and relax – and just before I fell asleep, I thought I could feel him smile.

Chapter Twenty

The sunlight woke me up. Paolo was gone, and the fire was out. I stood up and stretched. My stomach woke up too, and I listened to it growl. I looked around for the crackers.

There were not many left. I did not want to think about that. I reached for the door, wondering where Paolo was.

My eyes had to adjust to the light as I swung open the door and stepped out. It was cold. I stopped to lace up my shoes. There was something ghostly about this place. I listened to the wind that never seemed to stop, and could almost feel the spirits of ancient civilizations.

The altitude must have been working on my mind. Even in the sunlight, this was a scary place.

I stood up and walked around, looking for Paolo. I could have called out for him, but something stopped me from breaking the silence.

I moved away from the shack towards the mountain. If this was a mine, the entrance would not be far away. And if it was a mine, they must have some way of getting the ore down the mountain.

Tracks. There must be tracks. I was excited now, and began to walk faster. Close to the face of the mountain I almost stumbled over them. There were tracks here. We could follow them.

Staring at the ground I followed the tracks to the east. Around the bend on the other side of the peak was the opening of the mine and the end of the trail. And that's where I found Paolo.

I walked up behind him and tapped him on the shoulder. He jumped a foot, and almost fell off the mountain.

"Geez. Did you have to scare me like that?" he said angrily.

"Well, good morning to you, too. I'm sorry. I did not mean to scare you."

"I'm sorry I snapped at you. Look, Rose. Here is the mine."

"I can see that. The tracks are what I was thinking about," I said.

"Yes. Me too. We can follow them down. But there are places too steep for walking. See how the tracks are notched? This is so the cars won't slide down the steep places."

"If there are places too steep for walking, how do we get down?" I asked.

"Well, the mine was here before there were trains. The ancient people mined here also. They used trails and mules. The old trails are here too. We could follow the tracks until they get too steep, and then follow the trails."

"Sounds okay with me," I said.

"And we don't have to climb all the way down, only to the farm house we saw last night."

"Great. Let's go." I said, anxious to leave this place.

"Don't you want to see the mine?" He asked.

I looked at the entrance of the mine. It was just a hole in the rocks. No sign, no boards across the opening. Just an old cave. I knew caves were dangerous. There could be poisonous gas inside.

"Naw. Caves are dangerous. I'll wait for a tour. We have to get back home."

"Yes, but maybe there is something inside we could use," Paolo was edging closer to the dark opening.

"Paolo, what are you doing?" I said, pulling him back.

"I don't know, but I have to look," he said, twisting out of my grasp.

He ran ahead to the mouth of the cave. I wondered why they called it a mouth. I could almost see it swallowing up Paolo!

"Rose, come here." He called as he disappeared inside.

"Paolo. Come back." I yelled, running for the mouth as it sucked him in.

"It's okay, Rose. Look what I've found," came his disembodied voice.

I stopped at the dark opening. The sun was just high enough to light the entrance. My eyes adjusted to the dim light as I peered inside.

"Paolo? Are you there? What is it?" I asked.

Paolo's big, toothy smile greeted me as he stepped back into the light.

"We have a ride!" he said, waving his arm towards the old ore car parked inside.

"A ride?"

"Yes. It's an old ore car, and it has a brake. We can ride it down the mountain." Paolo said, with a wide grin on his face.

"No way! It's too dangerous! The mountain is too steep. We are not chunks of ore."

"We don't have to ride it all the way, only to the farm below. It has a brake, and we can stop it if we have to," Paolo smiled again. "It will be okay, Rose."

"Even if we could – and I'm not saying I would – how do we know we can stop it?"

"Well, they said the mine was closed for the winter. They must have been using this car not too long ago. The brake must be okay. We'll just have to take our chances." Paolo spoke with some authority in his voice.

I didn't like the idea of spending hours or days hiking down the mountain without food, and very little water, but I sure didn't want to take a roller coaster ride in an old mining car, either.

Paolo examined the brake, pulling it back and forth.

"We can do it, Rose."

There's a time for thinking, and a time for doing. Sometimes you can think too much.

"Okay, let's do it." I said. "Now, before I change my mind."

Paolo released the brake.

"Help me push it outside," he said.

We pushed the old car out into the light. It was heavy and we slipped more than once, falling onto the ground behind the old rusty bucket. Finally, it sat in the sun, held by the brake. We walked back to the shack, collecting our few, meager supplies.

"How do we get it rolling when we are inside?" I asked.

"There is a long pole inside the cave. I saw it standing against the wall. I'll get it." Paolo said running back inside.

I climbed into the old bucket. We would have to sit on the ends facing each other.

Paolo came out with the pole.

"Once we get started, I'll throw the pole away. Then I can work the brake."

Paolo climbed in.

Sheesh! I would have to ride backwards down the mountain. Not only that, I would have to look at Paolo all the way. I did not want him to know how scared I was!

"Here we go." He said, standing up, and facing backwards as he used the pole to push off.

He strained and strained – and very slowly the car started to move.

I stared at the sky and the mountain peaks. I saw an eagle in the clouds. I did anything I could to keep from thinking.

The car picked up speed, and Paolo threw away the pole. He sat on the edge, hand ready on the brake.

Soon we were rolling faster. The old shack we had stayed in passed in and out of my view. The butterflies were dancing in my stomach, and I vowed if I lived through this I would never ride a roller coaster again.

Chapter Twenty-One

"Susan, any news?" Mom talked to her laptop on Zip as the sun came up in Lima.

"Not since last night. All the Agency computers register the same tracking signal. It's almost like the perpetrators keep moving the kids around. On another note, though, we feel we are closing in on the mole. Seems a certain employee has ties to the Peru Mining Company, and pushed the proposal for the Peru Wire Company contract to the director. We're checking the officials at Peru Mining for possible terrorist connections. The company is partly U.S. owned and runs the copper mines in Cerro de Pasco supplying Peru Wire."

"That's where my research led, too," Mom said.

"We must be getting close to the answer, or they wouldn't have grabbed the kids," Susan said.

"We've been in touch with Richard, too," Mom went on, "Seems like our run-in with the Old Fox and the Shining Path wasn't just a coincidence. Oh, why did I let her go with Paolo?"

"I know the feeling," Susan remembered her decision to take me to New York that led to our kidnapping, "Has there been any contact or demands?"

"No, but we think the kids are probably safe. The tracking signal gives us hope. Apparently the kidnappers haven't found it yet. Besides, we think they will probably contact us today with instructions. Oh, why did we come here?" Mom was trying hard to be professional, but ran into being a professional mom.

"Don't do that to yourself," Susan said. "There's always going to be that danger whether you are home or not. The only way to avoid it would be to change our whole family history, and then the danger is still there. That's the kind of world we live in. That's why we are in this business, remember?"

"Yes, I know but I keep going around in circles. If only…" Susan cut off mom's last words, "Keep your chin up and we'll find them."

In the background, Samson barked as if to give Mom hope.

Dad was on his cell phone talking to Richard, "What news?"

"Seems, 'the Old Fox' has a protégé who was one of the four Shining Path members arrested in 1998 for urban terrorism in Lima. Last night he came to the Pizzaro club looking for his old flame. He had too much to drink, and went nuts when he saw me with her. He tried to slug it out with me, and landed right in the booth. Then he tried to impress her by talking about the 'glory' days in '98. Once his tongue started wagging, he went on to say the Old Fox was back in business again. Something big went down yesterday – but he wouldn't say what."

"It sounds like we're on to something." Dad said. "The timing is too coincidental. We must have gotten too close at the wire factory. Maybe the kids followed me, or maybe they were taken there."

"Right, that's where the last stationary signal came from. All the evidence is pointing to the wire company, and a plot to stall the Agency from upgrading their computers. But the question is, why?"

"To keep us from finding out what's coming – the next big terrorist attack. Where is the protégé now?" Dad asked with urgency in his voice.

"He's sleeping it off in a cheap hotel. I'm going to follow him today as a new recruit."

"Good. When we find the kids, we'll find the answers," Dad said.

A knock at the door interrupted the conversation. One of the Peruvian policemen swung open the door to escort Paolo's father into the room. He was holding a camera, my camera!

"Hold on, Richard, I think we got a break…"

"Hold on Susan, someone just came in…" Mom said.

Everything stopped as Pablo stood in the middle of the room holding the digital camera.

But nothing stopped where we were.

Chapter Twenty-Two

Where we were was picking up speed as we rounded the bend to the other side of the mountain. The ore car went faster and faster as the tracks wound down the far side of the peak. No wonder we hadn't seen them last night.

We hung on to the edges of the cart, trying to keep our balance. Paolo's face was contorted, and his mouth was wide open. All we could do was stare straight at each other; everything else was a blur.

The combination of being cold, hungry, and fifteen hundred feet up and rapidly descending in a roller coaster car was almost too much. I was sure we would barf on each other as the car bumped along, almost leaving the tracks.

Paolo's hand was frozen on the brake handle, and seemed unable to move. I couldn't see where we were going, and we had no idea how far the tracks went -- maybe all the way.

But they didn't. About a third of the way down the car hit a bumper, and we spilled out onto the ground, landing on top of each other, rolling into a pit -- a deep pit.

"Paolo, are you okay?" I asked, afraid to move.

"I think so," he said, "but I'm lying on the axe."

I had landed on top of him. Now that I knew he was okay, I rolled off, and helped him to his feet.

"What a ride! Where are we?" I asked.

"I don't know. It looks to be some kind of pit. Must be where they dump the ore to be picked up by the train." Paolo was looking around.

"Can we climb out?" I asked, trying to climb, but slipping back in on the loose rocks. The pit was about fifteen feet deep. I looked up at the rectangular patch of sky.

"It's too steep!" Paolo said, as he gave up trying to climb the steep sides.

"How will we get out?" I asked, leaning back against the side of the pit to rest.

"Do you still have the rope?" he asked hopefully.

"Yes! The bag fell in with us," I said, grabbing it, and pulling out the rope from the mining shack. "But what good will it do? There is no one to pull us out."

"We'll pull ourselves out!" Paolo said.

"How?" I asked.

"Like this!" Paolo said, tying one end of the rope to the axe and standing back against the far wall.

I was catching on.

"All we have to do is throw the axe until it catches something. Then we can use it like an anchor, and pull ourselves up!"

I found a safe place to stand as Paolo swung the axe and let go. It fell straight back down, and almost killed us.

He tried again. The axe was heavy, and he was not quite strong enough.

"It's no use. It's too heavy and there is not enough room to swing it," he said.

"Don't give up so easily. Let me try!" I said.

"If I can't do it, what makes you think you can? You're a girl."

"Big news, Mr. Smarty-pants – girls are strong, too!" I said angrily.

Getting beat by a girl must have given him the extra adrenaline he needed. With an anguished look on his face, he let out a roar of frustration, and flung the axe again.

This time it sailed out of the pit, and landed with a metallic 'clunk'. It had caught the wheel of the cart.

We both let out a laugh. "I'll go first!" Paolo said.

Testing the rope to see if it would hold, he dug his feet into the side of the pit. It held, and soon he was scaling the wall.

He scrambled over the top, one leg at a time, and rolled out of sight.

"Come on, Rose. Your turn." He said, looking down at me from the top.

I was glad I had learned to climb ropes in school.

Soon, we were both standing on the edge. We were a little scuffed up, but still in one piece.

"I think I know where we are!" Paolo said.

"Where?" I asked.

"Tarma! Or somewhere close to it."

"Where is Tarma?" I asked, trying to remember my research.

"It is one of the three passes across the Andes. There is a pass the Central Railroad takes from Lima to Tarma. It is about forty-eight meters high. About fourteen thousand feet. I watched the helicopter as we climbed the mountain. We must be near Cerro de Pasco. There is a mining company there, just north of La Oroya."

"Yes, I remember now. Most copper is mined in Northwest Peru. La Oroya is where the ore is smelted, but it is more central Peru," I said.

"But the train is not here. The pass is just opening up. We are still a long way up the mountain," Paolo sounded discouraged.

"The farm! We have to find the farm!" I said.

Gathering our supplies, we looked at the sun, and found our bearings. If we hiked south and west, we should be able to find it.

But hiking on the steep, narrow trails would be harder than it sounded.

Chapter
Twenty-Three

It was a little warmer now. Five hundred feet can make a difference! Since our kidnapping we had spent the last twenty-four hours in our windbreakers. Now we were hiking, and it helped to warm us up.

The rumbling in our stomachs kept us going. We had eaten the last of the crackers, and the remaining crumbs after our fall into the pit. A little snow was all we had, and we had packed the plastic water bottle with it.

Paolo still carried the axe he had fallen on. Now and then he would put his hand to his side. It was bruised badly. We had to stop and rest a lot. The altitude and our hunger had a lot to do with that.

We followed the tracks until they became too steep. The pit we had fallen into was on a spur, beyond the regular route of the Central Railroad. We had found the tracks for a small work train designed to pick up the ore from the pit, and take it to the smelter.

Unfortunately, the winter season wasn't over for the miners yet, and no trains ran up here. Nothing would happen until the pass was fully open. There were no phones, so we kept walking, using the trail the ancient miners used. It was designed more for mules and llamas than people, and over-grown with bushes.

More than once, Paolo had to use the axe to cut through the brush. The long handle did not help. Sometimes he used it as a crutch. My ankle was sore from the fall, and I thought of using it as a crutch too.

"Rose, you are limping! What is wrong?"

"I think I twisted my ankle back there in the pit."

"Let's stop and rest," Paolo said, looking for a rock or something to sit on.

The mountain was terraced, and we stopped at the next opening in the brush. We sat on the trail, and hung our feet over the side, looking at the mountains around us. At this altitude we could see the vegetation covering so many of the mountains here.

"They look green," I said.

"Yes. We are on a terrace. I think we are nearing the farm."

I remembered reading how the farmers grew their crops on the terraces. The pictures I had seen of Machu Picchu were like that.

"Paolo, how far is Machu Picchu?" I asked.

"A long way. It is to the east and south on the other side of Peru."

"Have you ever been there?" I asked.

"No. Some day I will see it, though. I know it is not going away. Were you not going to see it while you are here?"

"We were supposed to go yesterday. It keeps changing. Mom and Dad have to keep working. We will see it before we go home. If I ever want to see a mountain again. Why haven't you seen it? You live here."

Paolo smiled. "My father has to work. Can you walk?" He asked, getting to his feet.

"Yes, I think so," I said, standing and testing my left ankle. It was sore, and throbbing, but not as bad as before. It was probably only a minor sprain.

"It must be about noon. The sun is almost directly above us," Paolo noted.

"Let's get to work!" I said, picking up the canvas bag, draping it around my neck, and under my right arm.

Paolo picked up the axe, and we started back on the trail. Cutting through the brush, slipping on loose rocks, we headed south and west toward the 'farm'.

I noticed in the clear stretches how Paolo kept leaning on the axe handle and bending to his left. I knew he was in pain.

"Paolo, how is your side?"

"It is sore but it will be okay," Paolo said in a slightly strained voice.

"It doesn't look okay to me, maybe we should stop," I said.

"We will never get home if we do," he replied.

I watched the sun move lower in the sky. It stayed ahead of us, and the glare made it hard to see. We limped along, not knowing how far we had come, or thinking of how hungry we were.

As the sun moved lower, so did we. Our jackets were tied around our waists now, and we walked like zombies, one painful step at a time.

"Paolo, we have to stop."

"Yes, we must stop," Paolo said, zombie-like.

There was a rock with a large flat top ahead of us. We headed for it, slumping down on it as if it were a bed.

"Let me see your side," I insisted.

He said nothing, but sat still while I lifted his shirt. He cringed as the t-shirt slid over his ribs.

"Oh, Paolo!" I said, seeing the large, purple bruise covering most of his right side. He was having trouble breathing, too.

"I think this is more than a bruise. You might have broken a rib," I said, carefully lowering his shirt.

Paolo was sweating and looked feverish. I put my hand to his forehead. It was clammy.

"How is your ankle?" he asked.

"Sore, but I'll live."

"Me too."

There were only a few hours of daylight left now. I knew we had to find help soon.

"Paolo, stay here and rest. I'm going to look around."

He did not argue. I stood up and hobbled to the side of the trail.

Looking up beyond the brush, I could see the top of the mountain. We had come quite a ways but still were quite high. The canopy of trees and brush kept me from seeing much else and just as I was turning back to the trail; I saw a wisp of smoke.

"The farm!" I yelled, smelling the cooking coming from below. I knew it was not too far now!

Heart beating in anticipation, I ran back to Paolo ignoring the pain in my ankle.

The butterflies in my stomach came to a sudden stop as I approached the rock. Paolo had slid off of it and was slumped over on the ground.

"Paolo! Are you okay? Paolo, I found the farm. Paolo…"

This couldn't be happening! Not now! Not after all that!

"Paolo…come back. Come back…" I shook him again and again. Finally, I sat on the ground next to him and cried.

Chapter Twenty-Four

I must have fallen asleep. I remembered crying, afraid Paolo was gone. But he must be okay, I thought, his hand was on my shoulder trying to wake me up. My eyes were still closed, waiting for his voice.

The gentle shaking continued and I still did not hear him say anything. I opened my eyes, unsure of what I would see. Had the Old Fox found us? Was Paolo all right? I couldn't handle the curiosity. I opened my eyes, awake, and wary.

It wasn't Paolo shaking me, and it wasn't a hand either. It was a nose. A nose belonging to a young Alpaca. I sat very still, and thought back on my research. I remembered that alpacas were mostly found in the high plateaus of the mountains. As far as I knew, they were friendly and would probably not hurt us, though they did spit like llamas and camels. This one was brown, and his wool would be highly prized when he matured.

The nudging stopped when I opened my eyes and the alpaca stood back as if waiting for me to do something. I smiled. He just stood there, expectantly. I shook Paolo.

"Paolo, are you okay? Wake up," I whispered.

"Rose? What happened?" He asked, lifting his head from my shoulder, and wiping the sleep from his eyes.

"Shhh! Don't scare him away."

"Scare who away?"

"The alpaca!"

"Oh, oh!" He said, suddenly awake, and staring at our new friend.

"You must have had a fever; you passed out while I was scouting the trail. When I came back I found you on the ground. I thought you were dead," I said relief in my voice.

"I did not mean to scare you. The thin air must have gotten to me. I was so tired," he explained.

"I'm just glad you are okay!" I said, still whispering.

"What is he waiting for?" Paolo asked.

"I don't know. He almost acts like a pet or an animal that is used to people." It was too hard to keep whispering so I let my voice get a little louder.

"Rose! What if that is not a farm? I think it may be a ranch. Maybe they raise alpacas for their wool."

"That would make sense. Anyway, farm or ranch – it makes no difference. There are people there, and they can help us!"

"Maybe the alpaca can lead us there. We must be close!" Paolo was excited now, and struggled to his feet holding his side.

I stood up, too, expecting the alpaca to run, but he didn't.

We picked up our supplies, and turned toward the ranch. The smell of cooking was still in the air, and though the sun was getting low, we still had daylight.

The alpaca followed as we started walking, then ran ahead and took the lead on the trail.

We smiled, and followed him.

"I guess he is used to getting fed. Maybe he will lead us right to his pen," Paolo said.

And that is exactly what he did. We were happy not to be alone anymore, and the animal knew the trail. Soon the ranch was in sight.

The trail broadened. Soon it looked more like a road, and we were walking faster now. In the distance we could see a house, and two large fenced areas, one on either side of the road.

The light was fading now, and we could just make out shapes in the pens. Llamas and alpacas. There was a glow of firelight, and the sound of a barking dog coming through the window of the house.

It was a small dog, a border collie, most likely. The alpaca was immediately herded in the direction of his corral.

The dog was followed by another small figure, a girl. She was yelling something at the dog in Spanish, and stopped suddenly when she saw us.

I guess we would have been a surprise! Up here where few visitors ever come, especially two young children limping and carrying an axe!

We stopped. Paolo said something to the girl. Since I didn't know much Spanish, I relied on Paolo to translate.

"Her name is Maria," he said, as he introduced us. "I told her who we are and that we needed help."

"Si." She said motioning us to follow her as the dog ran behind us, nipping at our heels as if it was herding us.

"Peso!" She scolded the dog. "No, no!"

Peso kept herding us anyway, and we laughed as we followed Maria up to the door of her house.

Chapter
Twenty-Five

I would not have recognized Richard if I had seen him that night. He had let his beard grow since we had arrived, and was wearing an eye patch. A wig with a ponytail completed the look. The silvery gray shirt tucked into his black dress pants helped make him look like a successful drug dealer.

He was deep undercover and the news of our kidnapping gave him an anger that fit the character he was playing.

As Paolo and I were limping up to the ranch on the mountain, Richard was riding through Lima with his new 'friend'.

"Where is this place, Marcos?"

"You in a hurry?" Marcos said as he stepped harder on the gas pedal, almost running down the pedestrians in front of the bars.

"Hey, watch out!" Richard snapped. "We don't need the police bothering us."

"You talk like an old lady. Maybe my driving makes you nervous?"

"It's not your driving; it's you who make me nervous," Richard said, relieved Marcos had slowed the car down. He could see people shaking their fists in the rearview mirror.

"Okay, okay. I was just having some fun. You will see where we are going when we get there." Marcos turned the corner and headed towards the coast.

He did not see the small black car pulling out a block behind him with the lights off.

"So, you think they will like me?" Richard asked, trying to keep Marcos' attention.

"We are always looking for a few good men," Marcos laughed. "If I like you, they will like you."

Richard knew Marcos had fallen out of favor with the leaders of The Shining Path. He was the kind of man who wanted to act tough, and impress his peers. They used him accordingly. He was also the kind of man who drank, and talked too much. They used him for that, too. Whenever they wanted or needed to plant some red herrings they gave him false information and wound him up. Then they set him loose after plying him with alcohol.

Marcos knew what they were doing, but told himself he was useful. He traded his pride for the association and the booze.

Rico and Gloria knew about Marcos, and had suggested Richard contact him. They took Richard to the bar, and set up his room at the cheap hotel. Now they were following at a safe distance and listening to the conversation on Richard's COM link.

"A few good men; just like the U.S. Marines. That's funny," Richard said without laughing.

"You don't laugh, yet you say that's funny. Maybe you are funny," Marcos said as the car rolled along the dark highway.

"If I say it's funny, it's funny. Maybe you would like it if I laughed at you?" Richard's voice was threatening.

"Why would you laugh at me? Am I drunk? No, not tonight. People laugh at me when I am drunk. They say, 'Get Marcos, I need a laugh.' Then they send me out on a fool's errand. Are you playing me for a fool, friend?"

"If I was, would I tell you? No, if you doubted me, we would not be riding in your car. I am beginning to doubt you, though. Do you really know the Old Fox?"

"You see," Marcos, said, "you don't believe me. If I say I know the Old Fox, then I do."

"Okay, I believe you. Your joke was funny too," Richard laughed and broke the tension.

Rico and Gloria relaxed as they followed behind.

They finally came to a stop at the docks. Marcos parked the car and set the alarm. Richard followed him to a fishing boat.

Once on the boat they went below decks, and into the captain's cabin. There, three men, who did not introduce themselves, were seated at a small table.

"Marcos! Good to see you again! And this is your new friend?" one of them said, as he stood up to shake hands.

The other two nodded and smiled, but did not stand up.

"This is my friend, Crocker," he motioned to Richard and used his alias.

"And you are…?" Richard stuck out his hand.

"The man with no name," came the answer. "The rules here are no names."

Richard – Crocker – dropped his hand. "But you know mine," he said.

"We know Marcos called you Crocker. We have yet to know you. Until we do, we do not shake hands, or use our names. You don't just walk into this organization on the strength of a night's drinking."

The boat had pulled away from the dock, and was headed out to sea. Richard had expected something entirely different – a camp in the hills, or maybe a meeting in town.

When they arrived at the dock, he saw the possibility that maybe this is what happened to Paolo and me. The tracking signal on the booby bird had been over water at times.

"You are a smart man," Richard said. "I would not like to work with stupid ones."

"No, we are not stupid, Mr. Crocker. Right now your picture is running through our computer. If you are not who you say you are, we will know."

"And if I am?" Richard said.

"Sit down, Crocker. We will play cards. Do you like to gamble? Of course you do. You would not be here if you didn't."

"Cards?" Richard asked.

"You can tell a lot about a man by the way he plays cards. You pick the game."

"What are the choices?" Richard said, looking at the faces in the cabin.

"It could be poker or it could be go fish," the man smiled.

"I don't play cards with people who don't give their names," Richard said, as he stared at the faces in the room.

"A smart move, but you didn't get the joke."

"Oh, I got it; I just didn't think it was funny."

"He doesn't laugh at funny things," Marcos broke in.

"I don't trust a man without a sense of humor," the leader said, searching Richard's face.

"And I don't trust a man who laughs at another man's fate," Richard replied.

The men at the table turned their heads from one to the other as they watched the verbal poker game between their leader and Richard. Marcos was beginning to sweat. If they found out that Crocker was not who he said he was, both of them would die.

Dying was not the worst of it, though. First they would be tortured to find out who had sent them.

Richard knew that, too. He waited for the knock at the door. But he had an ace up his sleeve.

After all, you don't just walk into an organization like The Shining Path.

Chapter Twenty-Six

Richard was not the only one waiting for a knock on the door. Back at home Susan and Steven waited for their contact at the Agency.

"Why are we meeting at a restaurant?" Susan asked as they parked the car at the giant Mall of America.

"We can't trust the computer," Steven said as they locked the car, walking toward the skyway, and into the Mall.

The mall was always busy, and Steven seemed unconcerned about being overheard.

"I suppose you are right. Anyone at the Agency could monitor our communications. I just hope our informant has some information for us," Susan's frustrations were showing through.

Paolo and I had been missing for thirty-six hours, and both Aunt Susan and Uncle Steven were weary of Zip.

"I just wish we were here under different circumstances," Steven said as they found the restaurant on the map, and he checked his watch.

"Me too," Susan sighed. "This was supposed to be a routine investigation. I can't believe Rose is a hostage again."

"Well, now we're pretty certain the delay in delivering the wire is part of a terrorist plot. Maybe tonight we'll find

121

out what they are up to," Steven held the door for Susan, and they followed the host to a table.

They ordered drinks and waited for the contact to appear. Steven liked getting to a rendezvous early. It gave him the chance to scout the area – an advantage over his contact. He also liked watching the entrance.

A determined looking man approached the door and checked his watch. He held it up to his ear, and tapped the face of it twice. That was the signal.

Steven smiled and waved the man over.

"Well, *Fred*, good to see you. Thought you got held up at the airport. Any trouble with your luggage?"

"Steven, Susan. Good to see you, too. Yes, my suitcase was open," Fred said as he sat across from Steven and Susan.

"But, fortunately, the bag was zipped?" Susan said, giving the countersign.

"Yes, all my I.D. was in there. I was able to retrieve it, though. I'll tell you all about it while we eat."

Over dinner, Fred told them they had identified the mole, and watched him while they traced his activities. The noise of conversation, and clinking silverware made it difficult for anyone who might be listening in.

"Seems Mr. X is well connected. As you know, Peru Mining is partly owned by the U.S. Having worked as assistant to the president of the company, he was recommended for a similar job with the director of the Agency. He was hired almost two years ago, and his performance has been flawless. Once he gained the director's trust, it was a simple matter to slide the contract proposal from Peru Wire onto his desk. When the director asked him for his opinion on it, he said he thought it would be good for relations between the two countries. Not to mention the price, which was much lower than other supplier, and would help the Agency's budget. It all sounded good, and made sense – so the director approved it." Fred finished with a sip of his water.

"Seems so easy," Steven said, as 'Fred' took another drink.

"Yes. That's how they work. Right under our noses. Anyway, the director was under a lot of pressure from the White House. The president was taking a lot of flack for the information breakdown and the Agency pointed to the fifteen-year-old computer system. They needed to tell the public they would be updated in spite of budget constraints." Fred stopped to eat a few bites.

"Well, this latest incident will not help relations with Peru," Susan said.

"On the contrary, Peru is denying any involvement and is cooperating in the search and the investigation. They have vowed to find the people responsible, and are pointing to The Path. They believe there is an international conspiracy by the terrorists for an even bigger catastrophe than 9/11," Fred finally finished his dinner.

"What about the kids?" Steven said. "Do you think they are hostages?"

Fred pushed his plate away, and motioned to the waiter for another drink. He avoided looking at Susan.

"No. We don't believe the children are hostages. Rose's camera was found by Paolo's uncle. On it were pictures of the president of Peru Wire and The Old Fox, a member of the Shining Path. We believe they might have seen and heard too much."

Susan dropped her fork. Steven's face went white.

"We think they are still alive, though. As you know, Rose's tracking signal is still coming in. We think we've finally got a fix on it."

"Do you think they are hurt?" Susan's voice was barely a whisper.

"No. If they were, they wouldn't keep moving them. Right now there is a Seal team in motion. We'll find them, and bring in their captors."

"We have to go in!" Steven said. "We can't just sit here…"

"No, we need you and Susan here. There are lots of people looking for those kids, including their parents, and the Peruvian police. We need you to take the information on Mr. X, and the officials of Peru Mining and Peru Wire to find out what the plan is."

"Why don't you just arrest them?" Susan asked.

"No, they would just clam up. Obviously the whole plan depends on secrecy. It's better if we just watch them, and track their communications. I have a feeling it will all lead to the same place."

"Why are they keeping the kids alive if they know too much?" Steven said.

"Could be timing. Obviously the event is still a ways off and they don't want to antagonize the anti-terrorist squads too much. The kids are a problem to them, but they can't risk anything happening to them. If they turn up dead, it could hurt their plan. I think they are buying time by moving them around." Fred said.

"Makes sense. I hope you are right. I hope the Seal team finds them!" Susan was holding back her tears.

Chapter
Twenty-Seven

None of the fishing boats detected the submarine as it glided silently underneath them off the coast of Peru. Hovering near the bottom, it waited for the five Seal team members to return.

Pulled along by personal underwater craft, the team was nearing the shore. Each was wearing a special tracking receiver set to my COM link.

The operation was set for dusk, since this was the hardest time to see. The Seal team, wearing black scuba suits, arrived at the shore just as the sun was disappearing from sight.

It was also dinnertime, and most people were either eating or relaxing after the supper meal, and few were paying attention to anything. So no one noticed as they slid their underwater craft onto the remote stretch of beach.

There wasn't anyone around this stretch of beach anyway.

Using hand signals, they converged on a sand mound where the COM link signal had finally come to rest.

Where were the guards? Where were the kids? The signal was still coming in.

They looked around for a building or vehicle. There was nothing but mounds of sand, and a few sprigs of weed.

Looking at each other, guns drawn, they decided to storm the sand hill.

And that's when they woke the booby bird!

The startled bird flew up into the darkness, only to be shot at by five laser rifles.

The night vision goggles revealed the bird somehow managed to avoid being hit. But before it flew off, the goggles revealed the COM link attached to its leg.

"Cease fire!" The squad leader yelled.

"It's a bird! A booby bird!" One of them said.

"We're the boobies," another one added.

After searching the beach, the squad leader radioed in. "It appears the perpetrators have thrown a red herring at us, sir. They attached the tracking device to a booby bird! No wonder the signal kept moving around so much!"

"You mean the children are not there?" came the reply.

"There is nothing here, sir, except five very embarrassed Seals."

"Then we don't know if the children are alive or not."

"No, sir."

"Secure the area and return to base."

The squad leader looked at his team. Each one was thinking the same thing. First, were the children still alive? And second, if news of this raid ever got out, they would be the laughing stock of the entire Navy.

Back on the sub, the commander reluctantly picked up the phone.

There were a lot of anxious people waiting for news of the rescue, but the most anxious ones were the children's parents.

This was a call he hated to make.

Chapter Twenty-Eight

Mom and Dad had been pacing the floor of the suite. The news of the rescue attempt had given them hope we had been found. Neither had even wanted to think we might not be alive.

"Oh, why did I let her go?" Mom was still crying.

"That's about the one hundredth time you've said that, and it won't help the kids," Dad reminded her.

"I know, but what else can we do?" Mom said, wiping her eyes.

"We can have faith in Rose. She's a tough little kid. Those terrorists don't know what they've got their hands on. And Paolo. There is a smart kid, too. Somehow I know we'll find them, and they will be all right!" Dad was convincing.

"I hope that Seal Team finds them!" Mom said.

"They will. The signal is still strong. It's the longest stationary transmission they've received. If the kids are there, they will find them. We should be getting the call any minute now."

As if on cue, the phone rang.

"Yes, Commander?" Dad said as he picked it up.

Mom watched as Dad's hopeful look disappeared.

"I see," he said. "Thank you for calling." The phone dropped from his hand.

"What is it?" Mom was frantic.

"They didn't find them," was all dad could muster.

"Where was the signal coming from, then?" Mom asked in a frantic voice.

"A bird. A booby bird," Dad was in shock.

"A bird? How?" Mom was in shock.

"It was attached to his leg. He's been flying around from here to there ever since the kids disappeared."

"Oh no! That means they could be…"

"Don't even think it!" Dad said. "They must be alive. Rose would never have told them about the barrette, so one of the kidnappers must have been familiar with the Agency. He put the barrette on a booby to throw us off and buy time."

"Or, he took it after he…" Mom couldn't say it.

"No, if he knew who Rose was, then he would know about the investigation. So far their whole strategy has been to delay the Agency's upgrade of their computers. They have been stalling for time. The time they needed to get their plan in motion without being detected. They didn't expect Rose to show up and take their pictures, but they must not have known about the camera. Paolo's uncle found it in the street outside the wire factory where he dropped them off. My guess is they will stick to their plan. They put the Com on the bird to throw us off and buy time. I don't think they would risk killing the kids and having their bodies show up somewhere."

"I have to think you are right," Mom said, "but what do we do now?"

"Two things. First, we start all over with good, old-fashioned detective work. We put too much stock in the COM link, and they used it against us. We've wasted time. Second, we start searching for the men in the photos Rose took. Find them, and we may find the kids."

"Richard should be getting close to the Old Fox, by now," Mom said. "Susan and Steven are tracking the mole at the Agency. It won't be long before we tighten the noose on these terrorists."

"Right, now lets get to work and hunt down the kids!" Dad said.

"Where do we start? They could be anywhere! There must be a million people in Lima, and a million miles of ground in Peru!" Mom's voice sounded defeated.

"We have to use all of our resources. Call Rico and Gloria, and the Captain of the Peruvian Police. I'll get on Zip, and call Susan and Steven. Oh, and one more thing, find out where Vladimir is," Dad was barking orders left and right.

"Vladimir?" Mom said, looking at Dad questionably.

"Yes. Our friend from Porcel-Art is also Russian and the new President of Peru Wire," Dad replied.

"Our past comes back to haunt us," Mom said, thinking of Vladimir and the porcelain mines in Russia.

"Then it's time to lay old ghosts to rest," Dad said, picking up the phone, and handing it to Mom.

Mom took the phone and called Rico and Gloria.

"Rico, pick up Paolo's family, and bring them here."

And so the largest, quietest kid hunt in the Agency's history was launched.

Chapter Twenty-Nine

They had to keep our kidnapping quiet. They couldn't risk the terrorists changing their plans and they did not want to scare them into doing something drastic – like killing us.

They also knew the odds of finding us alive were better than finding us dead. So, Paolo's father and grandmother started spreading the word along with Paolo's uncle how the search for us had to be very quiet in hopes of keeping us alive. Everyone they knew was sworn to secrecy. No media were allowed and only word of mouth was to be used.

The Agency and my parents were working the same way, as were the police. This made it harder to get information. Even the Internet and e-mail were blocked. Descriptions and pictures were passed around, one person at a time. Questioning suspects was tough.

Dad returned to the place where the camera was found and started piecing the trail together with good old-fashioned detective work. He knew we must be alive, and waited for Richard to contact him.

Richard was waiting, too. On board the boat with Marcos and the leader of this little pack, 'The Man With No Name', Locked in a verbal poker game, he nervously sat hoping the right card turned up.

Someone handed the leader a note. He smiled and looked up at 'Crocker'.

"Well, Crocker. It would seem you are who you say you are. You have quite an impressive background. Drug smuggling, gun running – caught, but never convicted. We could use a man with your talents. And you play poker very well. You never broke a sweat. Now, that was either because you are who you say you are or you know something we don't. Either way you are a cool hand."

Marcos let out a sigh of relief. Now that his new friend was accepted, he had risen a tad higher with his peers.

Richard had stayed calm the whole time. The ace up his sleeve was the Agency and the Crocker identity. He knew what the terrorists would find when they checked his name.

'Crocker' was a code name taken from Betty Crocker; it meant something was in the oven. It had been set up for Richard for use when he was undercover. In this case the computer synthesized his current activities into an appropriate cover.

As soon as the name was typed into a computer, flags went up at the Agency, the source of inquiry was tracked and a whisper copter was dispatched to the location of the boat.

"Should we move in now, sir?" the pilot asked his commander.

"No, protocol is twenty-four hours. Give Crocker time to see what's cooking. We only break protocol if Crocker contacts us, or seems to be in imminent danger. We'll stay in the shadows, and keep him in sight."

Richard knew he had twenty-four hours to find us, and find out as much information as possible about the terrorists' plans. After that he would be picked up, and the crew arrested.

Now he had to be careful and ask the right questions.

All of this was taking place as Paolo and I followed Maria to the front door of the mountain farmhouse. The sun was setting into the red sky, silhouetting in the mountains. Peso was running behind us, herding us, and nipping at my swollen ankle. Paolo held his bruised ribs, and both of our stomachs rumbled.

Safety and food was here. Everything else would have to wait.

Maria opened the door and the smell of cooking flooded over us as several shocked faces turned towards us and froze.

A man, an elderly lady, an older boy, and a younger girl were seated at the table in the kitchen.

Paolo interpreted as Maria introduced her family in Spanish. Her mother was standing over the pot of stew on the stove, dishing up the food for each one.

"Madre de Dios. Maria, what have you found?" her father asked, standing up from his chair.

"Father, this is Rose and Paolo. They need help."

"What are they doing on the mountain? How did they get here? What has happened to them?"

"Set a place for them. We will eat and then ask our questions," her mother said.

Chapter Thirty

Maria's father cleared his throat, and there was immediate silence. I knew he was about to say something.

"You must forgive our manners; it is not often we have visitors here. I am Roberto Ricardo Garcia. This is my wife, Christina Maria, her mother Isabella Sanchez, my son Miguel, (he motioned for Miguel to stand) our daughters, Maria and Clarissa. Welcome to our home."

I could tell he was very proud of his family and home. Tradition was very important here, even in the presence of two strange children.

Paolo was not to be outdone, even though I had started to speak first. "I am Paolo Rodriguez, and this is my friend, Rose. It is a pleasure to meet you all."

Roberto and Miguel sat back down, and after prayers we all started eating some kind of delicious stew, and homemade bread. I had an idea what kind of stew it was, but I was afraid to ask.

"It is llama," Maria's mother said, as if she knew what I was wondering.

I was relieved both of Maria's parents knew English.

"The llama is very important to people here. For more than two thousand years the natives have used them for work, food, warmth, and milk. It is with much respect we serve this stew," Roberto said.

"I've just never had it before. It is very good," I said, trying to get the image of the animal out of my head.

"In Bolivia they raise beef. We only have beef when we go to the markets," Roberto added.

Paolo and I were so hungry anything would have been delicious.

While we ate, we learned how Maria's grandmother was half Spanish and half Quechua, one of the native peoples. She had inherited the skill of making the beautiful handcrafts decorating the dried brick walls of the ranch house. Some were blankets woven with the figures of llamas, while some had Aztec-like patterns and designs. She also made beautiful shawls and scarves of fine needlework.

Christina, too, made beautiful things from the wool of the llamas and alpacas. Maria was learning the crafts as well.

Each spring, when the pass opened, they would bring their wares to the market in Lima. Paolo was surprised to learn some were sold in his grandmother's shop.

"The name Rodriguez was familiar to me. How nice to meet the boy I have only heard about!" Christina smiled.

Maria also helped Miguel with the chores, feeding the animals and cleaning the pens, helping Peso herd them and doing some shearing.

Miguel was fifteen and becoming a man. He worked closely with his father and watched the transactions at the market where some of the llama were sold. They also rented both llamas and alpacas to occasional teams of geologists and people exploring the mines.

Clarissa was five and a handful for her mother, who worked from "sun up to sun set" taking care of her home and family as well as the animals and crafts.

"She never sits still! She is so curious about everything!" Christina said.

I liked Clarissa instantly.

When the table was cleared and a fresh log put on the fire, Maria's father turned the conversation to our predicament.

"We must find a way for you to get home. But first we will tend to your injuries."

Isabella took me to her bedroom and inspected my ankle.

"Hmm," was all she said.

"How bad is it?" I asked, not knowing if she could understand me or not.

She smiled and tried to reassure me, understanding my tone more than my words.

"Is okay," she said, as she wrapped it with a red cloth soaked in something that must have been medicinal.

I felt a tingling on my skin as the wrap was applied, and I felt some relief from the throbbing pain I had been trying to ignore.

Christina attended to Paolo, wrapping his side in a similar way. Pulling down his shirt, she said we must get some rest.

"We will find places for you to sleep tonight," she said.

Back in the main part of the house, we talked to Roberto and Miguel.

"We have no phone. The closest one is in Cerro de Pasco. The pass is opening, and the miners are coming back. Some of them live there all year long. The train will be running soon, and will take us to Lima. Cerro de Pasco is about one day from here. We will be leaving tomorrow to bring our wares to the market. Your timing is good. You can go with us. From there you can take the train to Lima," Roberto smiled and Miguel nodded.

The whole family was excited about the trip. Miguel had a far-away look as he talked about Lima. I suspected there might be more than just the big world waiting for him. He probably had a girlfriend he was mooning over.

Christina and Isabella joined us after putting Clarissa to bed. She hadn't wanted to go with the excitement of company here.

Mother and I will give up our train fare so you and Paolo can go home," Christina said.

"No, that wouldn't be right." I said, "You have waited all winter for this trip."

"I have money at home. We can repay you," Paolo said humbly but with pride.

"The right thing to do is to get you home," Roberto said. "We do not have much, but will share what we have."

"I will stay," Miguel said, straightening his shoulders.

"I will stay, too!" Maria added.

We were overwhelmed by their generosity. I felt bad for being a burden to them.

"I know lots of people are looking for us. You will be repaid…wait! Where is my canvas bag?"

Maria looked around. The bag was hanging on the wooden pegs by the door of the house. She went to get it.

She handed me the bag.

I reached inside and found the zippered pocket in the side of the bag. I unzipped it and reached in. My hand found the money tucked inside.

"Emergency money," Mom had said.

I counted the five twenty dollar bills, thanking my mother with every one. No one had to stay behind!

But there was something else we had to think about, the Old Fox and Alex Bacon, our kidnappers!

Chapter
Thirty-One

"What's wrong, Rose?" Paolo asked, seeing the look on my face.

"I was just thinking, what if the Old Fox and Alex have someone watching for us? What's in Cerro de Pasco? Will we be safe?"

Paolo talked with Roberto in Spanish.

Roberto nodded, "Si, the mining company is there. People are coming back with the end of winter. I have friends there, and family, it is where I grew up. We board our animals there when we go to Lima. We can disguise you. If those men are there watching, they will think you are part of our family. When we load our goods onto the train they will not notice you. There is a telephone at the train station. You can call your family and let them know you are safe."

"We will not let anything happen to you." Miguel said.

"Thank you all so much," I smiled, relieved we would not be alone.

"We must get a good night's rest if we are leaving tomorrow," Christina said. "Rose, you can sleep with Maria, Paolo can bunk with Miguel. We must rotate our baths. Rose, you can have yours first."

While we were talking, Miguel put a large pot of water on the wood stove. Off the little kitchen was a bathroom and though they did not have running water, this was a place where you could bathe and shave. There was a mirror and a cabinet for razors and soaps. Hand-made towels hung on wooden racks, and the room was warm and cozy.

The tub was just large enough for one person, and it was covered in white enamel. It reminded me of movies I had seen of the old west. It took several trips to the mountain stream outside to fetch the water. Everyone joined in on a bucket brigade, and soon the tub was half full. Then the hot water was poured in, and with the soaps and perfumes ready, it was a nice hot bath.

Mine was short but sweet. Isabella made the soap from llama tallow and used flower petals to scent the water. I relaxed as much as possible, and my ankle felt much better after a soak. Isabella wrapped it again when I was dry.

Everyone pitched in and we dumped the old water out and the process was repeated three more times, with the men interrupting their work for the bucket brigade. Miguel kept the pot full on the stove, throwing more wood into the fire when needed.

It was late night before the baths were finished and preparations for the trip were made.

"What about the guys? When do they get their baths?" I asked Christina, as we got ready for bed.

"They take their baths in the morning, in the stream," she said.

"Brrr! Isn't it cold?" I said with a shiver.

"Of course it is, but they will never admit it," she smiled and shook her head.

I wondered how I would talk with Maria as we climbed into the hand-made wooden bed. The woven blankets were

soft, and though the bed was small, it felt much better than
the floor of the old mining shack.

When we were all settled in, Peso jumped on the foot of
the bed. The little dog curled up between our feet, and made
me lonesome for Sam.

"You are sad?" Maria said. She could see my face in the
candlelight. She spoke some English.

"I miss my dog."

Maria nodded as she blew out the candle. She put a comforting arm around me, and we fell asleep in the moonlight
listening to the sounds of the mountain.

The night went fast. I had not realized how tired I was,
and the pain in my ankle must have given me dreams. It was
all a blur, but I was surprised how rested I felt as the sun
came up.

Morning came early and I woke to Maria prodding me to
get up. We had to wait in line to brush our hair and teeth.

I was not even awake yet, and already the house was full
of noise. Breakfast was cooking on the stove, and there was
an excitement in the air. This was a big day.

Outside, the noise of the llamas and alpacas and a barking Peso mixed with the sounds of laughter.

"So, Paolo, in the city you take warm baths, eh?" Roberto
smiled as he emerged from the cold mountain stream. It was
a cool morning at 14,000 feet. Miguel smiled at the 'city
boy', and then jumped into the stream to submerge himself
in the shallow water.

Paolo jumped right in after him. "I never had a hot bath.
We are not wealthy," he said, splashing water at Miguel.

It was cold, but like Christina had said, not one of them
would show it.

Of course, we could only hear them splashing. The bathing spot was secluded from sight.

Most of the work had been done the night before. Blankets were folded and piled. The pickup truck was stacked on one end with months of work. The girls and women had made woven mats, decorated blankets, wall hangings, scarves and fine needlework. The men had things to sell also.

Roberto had coils of rope braided from the long coarse hair from the llama. Miguel had made leather wallets and purses from tanned leather.

"Wow! This is intense! How did you make so many things over the winter?" I asked as we stepped outside to load the last few things.

"Most of what you see was made long ago. We are always making new things, and some things take much time. Not all you see was made this winter," Christina smiled.

"Of course, how silly I am," I said, blushing.

I remembered Dimitri's family in Gzhel. Once again I was reminded of the importance of art.

"My father carves driftwood. He is very good," Paolo announced.

"I would like to see it someday," Roberto said.

The front seat was reserved for the grownups to ride in. The rest of us had to find places in back; at times Miguel would ride on the running board, talking to his father as he drove.

When everyone was ready, Roberto called Peso.

"Peso, you stay and watch the flock. Protect the house while we are gone."

Though he wanted to go along, he knew he had to stay. He sat, tail swishing the ground as Miguel climbed on to the old truck.

With a whine and a groan the pickup started off.

"Come on, old girl; let's go," Roberto prodded the truck affectionately.

Chapter Thirty-Two

I watched my feet swing back and forth as we moved along the dirt road. Maria had lent me a pair of sandals and a red dress her mother had made for her. I wore it over my jeans. A matching jacket and a brown hat to hide my hair completed the outfit. My Reeboks were safely hidden in my canvas bag, and tucked under piles of blankets with Paolo's.

Paolo was also wearing a hat, and though his complexion was darker than mine, he still needed a disguise.

For my complexion, which was pale and freckled, Isabella had mixed up a special make-up. From a distance, I could pass for one of the family. If it worked once, it was all we needed.

I sat next to Isabella on the tailgate. Maria and Clarissa rode farther up in the bed, sitting on the load. We would take turns on the tailgate.

The morning sun behind us, we were headed west and slightly south. The road gradually got more narrow as we moved away from the ranch to lesser-used paths. The old truck seemed to have no problem negotiating the trail.

Maria wanted to know about my life back home. She had heard many stories of life in the United States. Yes, I thought, we are all rich and happy. To her, we would be. Hot water, telephones, television, and all the things she did not have would seem like an impossible dream.

There were other things she wanted to know, girl things that Paolo would have to translate. I was careful not to embarrass him too much. Besides, there are just some things boys don't need to know. Girls need their secrets.

We stopped for lunch, and I was grateful for the hat that helped to block out the sun. We had been driving away from it all morning and now it was above us. We would be facing it the rest of the day.

Finding a clearing next to the road, Roberto stopped. Christina and Isabella laid a blanket on the ground, and set up a picnic lunch. The men joined us, and we sat quiet for a while enjoying the view of the mountains.

"I've never seen such beautiful scenery," I said, eating a slice of homemade bread.

"You have never been in the mountains before?" Miguel asked.

"Yes, I've been in the Rocky Mountains, but the scenery is different. They are not green like these mountains."

"I have never been in the mountains," Paolo said, "I have always seen them, but my father is a fisherman. We live on the coast."

"I would like to go on a boat someday," Miguel said. "But I will probably take over the ranch."

"It must be a lonely life. How did you come to live on the mountain?" I asked between bites.

"My great-grandfather married Isabella's mother. She was a Quechua, and he was Spanish. She left her village, and they built a house on the mountain. My mother was born there, and one day my grandfather died. On a trip to Lima, she met my father. They wanted to get married, and

Isabella, with no husband to help her anymore, offered them the ranch. So, the rest of us were born there. I will probably continue the tradition. Some day we will have enough money to build and add modern conveniences to the ranch. I have big plans and the Internet and computers can help our ranch grow. Our first need is electricity." Miguel was excited about his dream.

"Cerro de Pasco is growing," Roberto said. "There are more year 'round residents and someday the town will expand. As it grows, the possibility for electric service grows also. Until then, we will have to use a generator. Fuel is expensive here, and we do not use it more than we have to."

"Yes, someday the world will catch up to us," Christina said.

Isabella rolled her eyes. She had liked the life she made, but like the day she left her village, she knew things would change. She was determined to keep tradition alive through her crafts.

Soon we all sat, nodding at the universal concept of family and home. I knew it was time to move on.

On our feet again, we picked up the blanket, and started up the engine.

The sun was finally behind us. We rode and talked into the evening.

Two-thirds of the way there we looked for a campsite for the night. It was too dangerous to drive at night. Once we found a suitable place, we set up a makeshift tent and started a campfire. Paolo and I helped gather the wood, and soon the crackling of a lively fire sent sparks drifting even higher into the air – sparks that led to smoke, and that smoke was seen.

"Where there is smoke..." The Old Fox lowered his binoculars.

"You don't think that is the children?" Alex said.

They had come to Cerro de Pasco suspecting Paolo and I might make it down from the mountain.

"No one lives on that mountain," the Old Fox said, raising the binoculars again.

"Maybe it is just tourists, mountain climbers, or explorers," Alex said hopefully. He had never been eager to kidnap the children in the first place. He was a businessman, and had been okay with his part of the plan, just to delay the wire.

"Maybe, but can we take that chance?" the Old Fox asked. The Path had a lot to lose if the plot failed, and much to gain if it succeeded. He was not above eliminating children for the cause.

"We don't even know if they overheard us, or what they know," Alex reminded him.

"I know who the girl is, though. She and her family are here for only one reason. Like her grandfather, they are not what they seem. I will not let history repeat itself," the Old Fox sounded angry.

"Revenge – is that what you really want?" Alex was angry.

"If this plan fails, the terrorists in the east will have their revenge, and it will be on us – possibly the whole world. If there is a chance those children overheard the plan, they must be silenced!" The Old Fox glared at Alex.

"Soon it will not matter what they know. The hour is drawing near for the event. They may never survive the mountain anyway," Alex was still angry.

"Fool! Do you not see how close they are getting? They are on the way to Cerro de Pasco! There they will find a phone, and the train! Once they contact their parents, it will be all over." Now the Old Fox had lost his composure.

"We will stay here and watch. When they arrive, we will stop them," the Old Fox had cooled a little; he lowered the binoculars, and turned. They were standing on the roof of the Peru Mining Company.

As the last of the sun disappeared they walked to the door and descended into the building. Watching the smoke from the fire, I wished I could send signals like the American Indians did.

Paolo sat studying my face. He got up and walked over to me. Sitting down again he put his arm around me.

"Don't worry, Rose. We'll get home."

"At least we found some nice people to help us," I said.

"Yes, who knows what kind of people we might have found," Paolo agreed.

Home, here I was sitting on a mountain half way around the world, I was as far from home as a kid can get. I recognized the queasy feeling in my stomach It was just like the feeling I had first felt when I was in far off Russia.

Would I ever get used to it?

Chapter
Thirty-Three

Morning found us on top of the blankets huddled together, Paolo, myself, Maria and Clarissa. The adults slept in the tent.

The smell of eggs and coffee on the campfire stirred us from sleep. I was happy we had not slept on the ground. We straightened and refolded the blankets then lined up for breakfast.

In spite of our situation, it had been fun. I couldn't help thinking what my parents would say when we got back. I would even take being grounded again just to be home.

But we had something important to tell them. Something important enough, to have us kidnapped and stranded on a mountain. We knew their plan. I wondered what was going on below. Of course, our parents and the Agency would be searching for us, and trying to uncover the terrorist plot. How much had they learned?

And time was running out. I couldn't wait to get to a phone in Cerro de Pasco. Things were happening back at home.

"You've got to call him now." Steven said to the hologram of the director.

"I know, and you're right. We should have done it sooner. The delay in the wire has been an embarrassment, and a strain on the Agency's relations with the president. But you've got to understand, careers are on the line." The holograph pleaded.

"Careers? There are thousands of lives at stake! And now two children who just might hold the key to the terrorist plot! A couple of twelve-year-old kids who managed to do what all your sophisticated equipment couldn't!" Susan was angry and Sam growled.

"Up until now we haven't had any hard evidence to share with him," the director smiled.

"We have enough evidence to arrest the mole, Alex Bacon, and the whole Path if we want to! Bring them in – and make them talk!" Steven's voice was rising. The hologram image vibrated from the tension.

"We can't just arrest a whole country on the basis of two missing children, and a photograph. International relations are touchy. We need the details of the plan: time, dates, and targets!" The director fought back.

"Our best chance of getting that kind of information is to find the kids. Still worried about your career? If the terrorists carry out a major strike, you won't have a career left to worry about. And if I find out we could have saved the kids, *and* stopped the terrorists you'll have more to worry about than just your career." Steven was shouting now and Sam was sitting up and barking.

Zip almost lost the image quivering under Steven's voice.

"We don't work for you anymore," Susan said, "if you don't call the president, we will. We'll get him to authorize the arrests."

"Okay, okay. The Agency will authorize the arrests, but not for twenty-four hours. We have to give Crocker the standard time before we move in," the Director sighed.

"You mean you need twenty-four hours to put a spin on things, don't you?" Susan said sarcastically.

"You know the procedure. The suitcase is closed," the director disappeared.

Susan looked at Steven. "I'm sure glad we got out when we did. Rose's dad was right to make a move to the private sector."

"Yeah, those budget cuts were a dangerous thing to do. Most of the senior agents are gone now, and the young lions are lost without their computers," Steven replied, stroking Sam's ears.

"Well, there are two lion cubs out there that didn't need a bunch of computers to find out what's been going on. I know they will be safe until the event takes place. A couple of aces in the hole," Susan hoped she was right.

"All we can do now is wait for Crocker. I hope he can find out where the kids are," Steven echoed the thoughts on everyone's minds.

Sam was pacing the Ready Room. All he could do was bark.

Richard was pacing, too. What was wrong? His Crocker I.D. had been accepted, and he was told he could meet the Council of The Shining Path. He had been hoping to see the Old Fox. Instead they had taken him to this little room, and told him to wait. That had been hours ago.

Finally, the door opened.

"Marcos! What's going on?" Richard asked as his new friend stood in the doorway.

"Come on. They want us on deck," he motioned with his hand for Crocker to follow.

"It's about time!" Crocker said.

He followed Marcos up the steps to the deck. There the 'leader' and his companions stood with smiles on their faces.

"Crocker! Marcos! So nice you could join us," he said, smiling.

"What is going on? I come offering my services, and you treat me like a prisoner! When do I get to meet the real boss?" Richard said angrily.

"Why is that so important? A job is a job..." the man with no name replied.

"I only deal with the top card," Crocker said. "I thought we were going to meet him."

"How do you know you haven't?"

"Because he would have told me he was, once he checked my identification," Richard did not want to tell him he would have recognized him.

"There are only two people in this organization who are stupid enough to brag about it, and Marcos is one of them, the other has made another unscheduled trip," The leader said.

"An unscheduled trip?" Crocker went fishing.

"Yes, his actions were never sanctioned by the Council, but we have to stand behind him to protect the cause. So he went to tie up a couple of loose ends."

Richard's heart was pounding. Was he talking about the kids? He had to control his anger and his excitement.

"Loose ends?" Crocker asked.

"Yes, like shoelaces, you can trip on them. Loose ends are dangerous."

Something changed in the air. Marcos started to sweat and Richard looked around. Twelve hours had gone by since they boarded the boat, and now the morning sun was glinting off the water. There was no land in sight.

Relaxing a little, Crocker smiled. Surely they would not do anything in broad daylight.

"Yes, I understand. In my business I cannot afford loose ends either."

"Then you will understand this."

Without warning, the men rushed Crocker and Marcos, knocking them against the side of the boat, and dumping them overboard.

Bobbing in the water, they began dodging bullets.

"Dive!" Richard yelled, grabbing Marcos and pulling him under.

The bullets followed them down.

Chapter Thirty-Four

Marcos was not a swimmer. Richard had to work hard to pull him under the surface, and keep him there. In the process his Crocker wig came off, and floated back up to the top.

The bullets kept coming, following the air bubbles from the struggling men. Finally, Marcos settled down and held his breath. Richard did not know how long he could hold his own. He only hoped it would be long enough for the shooting to stop.

He didn't dare look up for fear of rising to the surface again. He listened for the sounds of bullets in the water, twisting and pulling Marcos with him as they came.

Suddenly, the shooting stopped.

"Look! There he is!" One of the men on the boat saw Crocker's wig.

The shooting started again, and the wig was riddled with holes. Finally, it sank under the water, out of sight of the shooters.

"Let's go. They are dead and drowned," the man on the boat said.

Richard heard the boat churning away, and soon the water was quiet.

Lungs about to burst, he let out some air and started upward with the near-unconscious Marcos in tow.

Breaking the surface, they both gasped for air. Richard looked around, and saw the shredded wig, thankful for the disguise.

The boat was nowhere to be seen, and he knew they had narrowly escaped death. But now what to do? They were stranded in the middle of nowhere, floating in the water with no land in sight.

Richard reached up to the cross around his neck. Worn under his silk shirt it had helped complete the look of the drug dealer he had been playing. He prayed and pressed the back of the cross between his thumb and forefinger.

Would the tracking signal still work?

Still hidden underwater near the coast, the Seal Team sub had been monitoring communications with The Agency.

"Sir, we have a signal. It's Crocker's pick up call," the sonar man informed the captain.

"Coordinates?" the captain responded. "Let's not keep the good Crocker waiting."

When the coordinates came in, the sub came alive.

"Right full rudder, give me full speed ahead. The Seal Team prepare for rescue."

"Pray for me, too," Marcos gasped, dog paddling to stay afloat.

"Don't worry. Help is on the way," Richard said, letting go of the cross to fan the water.

"Who are you and what happened to your hair?" Marcos asked.

"You'll find out soon enough," Richard replied. "Save your energy."

"Sir, a message from the sub," the aide said as he rushed into the director's office.

With mixed emotions the Director read the message.

"The oven is open. Crocker is served," was all it said.

"Get me the president."

"Yes, sir," the aide walked to the phone.

"Sir, I have the Commander-in-Chief on the line."

"Good afternoon, Mr. President. I need to brief you on current events…"

"Sir, a message from your wife," the Peruvian police officer said as he left his car after talking on the radio. He walked over to Dad, who was interviewing local residents in the streets surrounding the wire factory.

Was it good news or bad? Was it about the kids? So many possibilities rushed through his mind as he walked with the officer back to the car.

Susan and Steven paced the Ready Room. Still upset with the director, they wondered if he would call the president now that Richard had come back in. They were grateful he was alive and well.

"It's a good thing you didn't let Sam bark while we were on hologram," Steven said.

"Yeah, his bark is like thunder. Usually only Rose can keep him from barking. She showed me how to do it once," Susan replied.

"What, is it kind of like keeping a sneeze from happening?" Steven said.

"Yeah, something like that," Aunt Susan smiled.

"Never works for me. Eventually the sneeze has to happen," Steven said, sniffling as if he had one coming.

"Oh no. Not that." Susan said in alarm.

"Ah, ah, ah, CHOO." Steven's feigned sneeze had become a real one.

The force of the sneeze penetrated the Ready Room and reached Samson's ears. A noise like thunder ripped through the neighborhood, vibrating the bunker door of Richard's Ready Room.

The barking continued until Susan made it outside in an attempt to quiet the furry giant.

"Eventually it has to happen," she said, putting a careful hand over Samson's nose.

"Eventually, it has to happen," the Old Fox said to Alex as they approached the telephone pole outside the Peru Mining Company.

"Once a plan is set in motion nothing can stop it. The Path has too much at stake to just back out," he continued.

"We have done our part. The hard line communists have put me in these offices to cooperate with the anti-U.S. interests. We have a large stake in this event also. But I do not agree with killing the children. Every plan must have a back-up plan, and killing the children would be bad for public relations after the event," Alex remained firm.

"You are in my country now. I will give the orders," the Old Fox was equally firm.

"I will go as far as delaying the children, kidnapping them again if we must; as long as the event takes place, all parties will be satisfied."

"Then help me cut this wire. We must not allow them to call home."

"E.T. phone home." The famous line from an old movie played in my head as we approached the town of Cerro de Pasco.

"I saw that movie!" Paolo said as the truck bounced along, garbling his words.

"We have to get to a phone!" I said, kneeling on the pile of blankets to look ahead over the roof of the truck.

"First one we see!" Christina shouted as we pulled into the outskirts of the town.

"There! Stop there!" I yelled, jumped out of the truck and ran to a phone booth alongside the street.

The truck squealed to a stop, and everyone jumped out, surrounding the booth.

"I hope it works," I said as I picked up the receiver.

"A dial tone! Hello, operator..." I started to say then stopped in mid-sentence.

The look on my face must have told everyone what happened.

"It's dead. Just went dead." I was in shock. "Someone must know we're here!"

Paolo shook his head. "No. We are so close!"

No one spoke. Little Clarissa, who had been so quiet sleeping most of the trip, put a hand to her face.

"Ah, ah, ah..." she stopped. There was a sneeze coming on.

I reached out and put a finger to her nose. It reminded me of how I would get Sam to keep from barking.

"A sneeze is like a bark," I said. "Once it gets started, it is hard to stop."

Clarissa looked up at me, and smiled. Sneeze averted!

I smiled back and took my finger from her nose, grateful for the distraction that kept us from panicking about the current events.

The smile quickly faded from her face.

"Ah, ah, ah, CHOO!"

Chapter Thirty-Five

"I know they are here," the Old Fox said as he put the wire cutters in the trunk of the rental car.

"How do you know?" Alex asked.

"I can feel it."

"What do we do next?"

"First we stop them from communicating their information; then, we must stop them from getting home. The event is only two days away. If we can keep them from talking, all will be well. The terrorists will get what they want; the Path will get what they want. Your friends will also. Everyone who knows the plan is sworn to secrecy, except those two children."

"How do we find them?" Alex asked. "And how did they manage to escape and get this far?"

"They must have had help. There must be someone on the mountain we did not know about, someone from Cerro de Pasco, maybe a miner or farmer. If the children have told them, they must be silenced also."

"How do we do that?"

"Really, Alexis! How did you get to be an executive? We kill them, of course. Eliminate the competition."

"I don't like it. Too much killing."

"And just what do you think will happen when the plan is executed? It is much too late to think about your qualms. A few lives are nothing added to the thousands you signed on for," the Old Fox was disgusted with Alex's lack of courage.

"But the plan seemed so remote, so far away," Alex's voice went quiet.

"So, killing is okay when you can't see your victims? Like a far off war?"

"Yes, like a war. For a cause," Alex was sweating now that he was closer to the events they had talked about. It was no longer an abstract idea.

"Enough! It falls to you and me to deal with this situation. There is only one way out, and that is to die. Do you wish to die?" The Old Fox's voice sounded menacing.

"No. I do not wish to die," Alex hung his head. He knew he would do whatever had to be done. That is how he got to his position, after all.

"What do we do next?" he asked the Old Fox as the Old Fox turned the key, and started the car.

"We must find them. I believe they will take the train to Lima. We must get to the station and find out when the next one is due. We must be there when they get there," the Old Fox said as he put the car into drive.

"They know we are here," I repeated as we all climbed back into the truck.

"How do you know that?" Paolo asked.

"The phone going dead was no accident. They must have been watching, and seen our campfires. They must have been worried we would escape the shack, and find a way off the mountain in time to warn the Agency. Remember, the Old Fox wanted to kill us, but Alex – Alexis – would not let him. They must have had second thoughts."

Chapter Thirty-Six

"The wire company gets the copper from Peru Mining." Roberto said, "This man, Alexis, must be connected with them also."

"Yes, I think so. Time is running out. There are only two days left until the terrorists carry out their plan. We must get word to the Agency!"

"How?" Paolo asked. "They have cut the phone lines. What will they do next?"

"They will try to find us and keep us from getting off the mountain. We must get to the train!"

"Si." Roberto said, climbing into the driver's seat and starting the old truck.

"Hold on to your seats!" he yelled as the truck lurched forward.

The gears growled, and the old pickup jumped with every shift. Soon we raced down the streets of Cerro de Pasco, the transmission giving off a high-pitched whine. It was the fastest this old truck had gone in a long time.

"Ahh, Ahh, CHOO." Clarissa sneezed again, and fell off her pile of blankets into Maria's lap.

"This is like a race," Maria said as the truck bumped along.

"I just hope we can win it!" I replied, grabbing the rolled edge of the metal box.

Clarissa sneezed again.

"It must be the dust from the road," Miguel said.

"The tires are kicking up a lot of it!" I said.

"Yes," Miguel replied, "this old truck is nothing to sneeze at.

"Time is running out," Dad said. "Whatever the terrorists have planned will happen soon – I can feel it."

"That means we have to find the kids soon," Mom said. They were talking on Zip to Steven, Susan and Richard on a three-way conference call.

"We may have a break," Susan said, "Seems Alex Bacon was recently named CEO of Peru Mining also. No coincidence, I'm sure. His ties to the hard-line communists suggest the terrorist event may be a joint project with other enemies of the U.S."

"Lately he has been seen in the company of the Old Fox. It seems The Shining Path has an interest in wire, too." Richard said from his window on the laptop. "I found out the old guy had to make an unscheduled trip."

"Yes," Dad said, "the staff at the wire factory said Alex was at a high-level meeting, and couldn't be reached. My guess is the mining company in Cerro de Pasco."

"Could be where they are holding the kids," Mom said hopefully.

"Should we send in the troops?" Steven asked.

"No. We don't want to endanger the kids. Our best chance of rescuing them is to not tip our hand. Besides, we still don't know what the target is. If we rush to get the kids, we may jump-start the event," Dad was trying to stay cool and professional.

"We could send Rico and Gloria. Their tour car is a good cover and would probably go unnoticed," Mom suggested.

"No, they can't take the car. There are only a couple of ways to get there and that's by train or plane," Richard pointed out.

"Let's put them on the train. They would not be conspicuous and a plane or chopper may alert the bad guys," Dad said.

"One good thing," Richard spoke, "the leader on the boat said the Old Fox was acting alone. Chances are it is just him and Alexis we have to deal with."

"Good. That gives the kids a better chance. Keep searching for clues to the terrorist plan, we'll contact Rico and Gloria and send them in." Dad's voice showed excitement.

"Just got some intel from the Agency; seems the phones are down in Cero de Pasco," Susan broke in.

"Well, it looks like we are on the right track!" Mom said.

The train was at the station when we arrived. We parked the pickup truck and loaded the goods onto a cart for the freight car. I felt clumsy in my disguise and worried about my hat falling off. I was sure we were being watched!

Paolo was used to this kind of work as he had often helped his grandmother unload blankets and handcrafts for her shop. He looked like one of the family.

No one seemed to be paying any attention to us as we loaded the car but still I could not shake the feeling that the Old Fox and Alex were there. I tried to look around without being conspicuous.

There were several families, businessmen and tourists. Not much different than people who wait for a bus in my country or people at an airport.

This was the first major run of the season with the pass opening up. Maria's family made this trip every spring and fall.

Still, I didn't see anyone who looked suspicious. The conductor talked about the phones being down and no way to communicate except the radio on the train.

If only I could get a message out. Of course, that is exactly what the Old Fox wanted to avoid. If I tried, I would blow our cover. I decided to get on the train and try to get us to Lima. I had given Roberto the money to buy tickets for Paolo and me. I thanked my mother silently again for putting the money in my canvas bag.

Maria's family kept an eye out for us too. I relaxed a little and finally put my bundle into the car.

And that's when my shoe fell out.

"There! That family loading the freight car! That shoe looks familiar. The girl, Rose, was wearing those shoes in the Plaza. She must be wearing a disguise!"

The Old Fox and Alex were parked around the corner from the station, using binoculars when no one was looking.

"What do we do?" Alex asked, lowering the binoculars and handing them back to the Old Fox.

"We could get on the train and try to grab them all. But that would mean we would have to hijack the train, and give ourselves away. The kids are obviously under the protection of the family they are with. We could follow them to Lima and try to stop them there, but the risk is too great. We have to make sure they do not talk to anyone." The Old Fox was trying to think fast.

"What about the radio on the train? Or in the station? One message is all it would take, and we would have the

Agency here in little time, or in Lima waiting for us." Alex was starting to sweat.

"Yes, you are correct, Alex. Let them think they have safely boarded the train. They will not try to radio anyone soon. They will think they have avoided us, and wait until they get to Lima. We will make sure they never arrive!"

Alexis was shocked. "What do you mean, never arrive?"

"There is some dynamite in the trunk of the car. We will get ahead of the train and plant it on the tracks!"

Alex's face went ashen; he couldn't believe what the Old Fox was suggesting. "No, you can't do that, what about all the women and children on the train? They are innocent people."

"Casualties of war. It is regrettable – but do I need to remind you again of our part in the plan? Millions will die, and economic chaos will break out in the U.S.! What is one train?"

"No! I won't be part of this!" Alex was firm.

"Then I will simply kill you now and do it anyway," the Old Fox was cold and Alex knew he meant what he had said.

Alex hung his head and mumbled to the Old Fox. "Okay. Then let us do it quickly!"

We found our seats as the train pulled out of the station. Thankfully, nothing suspicious had happened. It almost seemed too easy, and I remembered what Susan had once said in New York, "If something seems too easy, watch out!"

"Rose, you must tell us all you know," Roberto said. "If something happens at least more people will know, and someone will be able to get a message out."

"He is right, Rose," Paolo said.

I had avoided saying too much to Maria's family. I had not wanted to put them in danger. But after all that had happened, it seemed like right thing to do.

I gave them as much background as I could, and finished with the plan we had overheard at the wire factory just before we were kidnapped.

"We must get to Lima, and alert your parents. We must stop these madmen." Roberto said.

The Brooklyn Bridge and The Golden Gate Bridge? I thought you said there were three targets," Christina asked.

"The third target is symbolic. They plan on bombing three casinos in Las Vegas. All of this is set to happen at the same exact time the day after tomorrow. It has all been planned by word of mouth for the last few years, ever since the 9/11 attacks on the Twin Towers. Each cell or member of the plan had a specific job to do and delaying the wire needed for the Agency's new computers was an important part of the plan. It would help delay the coordination of information to tip off the authorities to the plan. My family was sent to Peru to investigate the hold-up in the delivery of the wire the Agency had contracted for. Whew! I lived up to my nickname on that one!"

"But if the U.S. is on alert, how will they avoid detection?" Miguel asked.

"Well, there is a battle going on at the airports for a better system of profiling travelers. Some people want to adopt the European system, and some people complain about privacy. The terrorists use this to their advantage. They know the holes in the system. As far as the actual bombings, unsuspecting people will carry them out.People driving to work, will not know their car is carrying a bomb. Tourists traveling to Vegas will not know their luggage has been tampered with. Once, I remember someone tried to blow up the Brooklyn Bridge. He was profiled and identified. Al-Qaeda had trained him. He was stopped. Now they figure no one would make a second attempt on the bridge."

I did not care who was listening now, and most of the passengers were. The looks on some of their faces were skeptical, though. Just a child's imagination.

Everyone was silent for a few minutes, digesting all that information. The train rolled along steadily, and we looked out the windows, wishing this were just another routine train ride into the city.

I watched the scenery flash by as the train picked up speed. We were traveling down the mountain now, and in a few hours we would be safe in Lima.

But hours were precious now. I wondered if there was a way to get to the radio in the engine car.

Just as I thought of it, I saw the black car on the road alongside the train. It seemed to be racing us.

The two men in the car looked familiar.

Chapter Thirty-Seven

"In that car!" I said. "It looks like the Old Fox and Alex! I think they are trying to beat us to the crossing!"

"But why?" Paolo said, climbing over Maria to see out the window.

"They're trying to stop the train!" I think I said it a little too loudly. The passengers were all crowding over to the left side of the train. Panic was growing! The conductor headed for the engine to tell the engineer.

Up front, the engineer hadn't seen the car yet. Everything was humming along normally, just another routine trip to Lima. "This job could get boring," he thought.

He checked his watch, proud of his record for being on time. Well, here was something to accomplish, anyway.

The black car sped ahead, finally catching up with the speed of the train, and then passing it! Alex was behind the wheel.

"Well, Alex! I see you have come to your senses!" the Old Fox smiled.

"Yes, we must beat that train!"

"We will! When we reach the crossing, stop the car in front of the track. I'll jump out and plant the dynamite!"

Alex just nodded and kept his foot on the pedal. The pedal was on the floor!

"Rose! We must stop the train!" Roberto said, reaching for the emergency cord.

"No!" Miguel stopped his father. "Not at this speed! We may all be killed by the sudden stop."

"He is right," one of the passengers shouted. "The black car cannot stop this train anyway. The men in the car will be killed, but we will be okay."

The time for action had passed. There was nothing we could do now but brace ourselves for the impact. I had seen the news story on television about how long it takes for a train to stop. And I had seen what a train could do to a car!

I hoped the conductor would reach the engineer in time, but in my heart I knew we could not do much. I was more worried about what the men in the car might do. I did not believe they would kill themselves by putting the car in front of the speeding locomotive.

"What is it, Rose?" Paolo asked, noting the change in my expression.

"I don't think they are going to try to stop the train," I said.

"Then why are they racing it? What do you think they are going to do?"

"Well, mining companies use explosives, right?" I said, not wanting to come right out and say what I was thinking.

"Yes, so?" Paolo was catching on. His voice was shaking a little.

"I think they are going to blow it up." I whispered, finger to my lips.

The engineer looked up from his watch. The track ahead looked clear. They would be approaching the crossing soon.

Almost time to blow the whistle! Blowing the whistle was his favorite part of the job. Usually no one was around to blow it at. Sometimes kids would be at the crossing, playing a dangerous game of daredevil, but no one had been hit yet. Once in a while a car would try to beat the train across the tracks, but that had not happened for a long time. "This will probably be just another whistle blower," he thought.

Being in the third car back, the conductor had to open the door, and walk to the other car. He walked through that car, trying to calm the passengers as he hurried up front. One more car to go. He hoped he would reach the engine in time. The black car was passing the engine now, approaching the crossing ahead of the train.

"Faster, Alex!" the Old Fox shouted. "I must have time to plant the dynamite!"

"My foot is on the floor!" Alex shouted back.

The car finally passed the engine and the Old Fox unbuckled his seat belt and unlocked the door. It looked like they would have just enough time.

The engineer reached for the whistle cord. He blew the approach signal. Outside at the crossing, the familiar 'ding-ding-ding' sounded as the striped arm lowered and the red stoplights flashed.

Two more blasts of the horn and they would sail across the intersection.

Just then, a black car came to a screeching halt in front of the arm at the crossing. A man jumped out of the car, and ran to the trunk – opening the lid just as the conductor burst into the engine compartment.

Suddenly, nothing was routine.

Alex sat at the wheel, the car's motor running. Just seconds now. Only a few seconds were left to determine the fate of so many people. Outside, the Old Fox had grabbed the dynamite, he was lighting the fuse and running to the tracks.

The engineer blasted the horn. Knowing he could not stop, he pushed the engine faster. Maybe they could plow right through it.

Inside the cars, there was panic. We were helpless. There was nothing we could do but pray! I looked at the frozen faces of Maria and her family. Somehow, I felt responsible for all of this. Why hadn't I listened to my parents?

"We'll be okay, Rose. We all will. I have prayed to Saint Rose of Lima." Paolo said.

I remembered reading about Saint Rose in the church I had toured with Mom. She was a Roman Catholic nun who lived from 1586-1617. She was born in Lima and became a nun in 1606. She became famous for the austerity she practiced, and was the first native-born saint of the Americas. I felt a connection with her name.

"It will take a miracle to get out us of this!" I said, hoping for one.

The Old Fox was holding the dynamite. Ignoring the screaming whistle, he turned around, facing the engine, and looked at the engineer for a second.

Alex had the motor running. He put the car in gear just as the Old Fox was turning toward him. He stepped on the gas.

Instead of going in reverse, the car lurched forward; blasting through the wooden arm, and hitting the startled Old Fox, pushing him – and the dynamite across the tracks just before the train flew by.

There was an explosion as the dynamite blew up in the Old Fox's hand. The car went up in flames as the gas tank exploded, and we could see it out the train windows as we rolled safely by.

Alex had made his decision.

Chapter Thirty-Eight

"Sheesh! That was too intense!" I said, sitting back down. The passengers all breathed sighs of relief, and then sat quietly in shock of what had just happened.

Christina was the first one to break the silence. "I made a lunch. We should eat."

It seemed strange to eat at a time like this, but it also seemed like the thing to do. I thought about it while she passed out the homemade fajitas.

"Mom, why do people eat at wakes? And what is a wake?" I had asked at my grandparents' funeral.

"We eat to bring normalcy back into our lives. Life goes on even after someone we love dies. We must go on," she said sadly.

"But why do we have a party?" I asked.

"It's not really a party. When someone faces death, people gather around, and surround the family with life. We need support and comfort. Food is something that brings people together. It gives them emotional strength as well as physical strength. We go through a lot of stress, and we need energy. Besides, we need to celebrate life – and let each other know our loved ones are not really gone, just somewhere else."

Well, I wondered who would miss the Old Fox and Alex. But we were still alive after a close call! That was reason to celebrate! Food never tasted so good! Normalcy.

Besides all that, Peru was a country used to chaos. There had been wars and struggles throughout its history. The people on the train were quick to return to normalcy.

But I suspected they would talk about this trip for a long time!

Back in Cerro de Pasco, Rico and Gloria stood outside of Peru Mining. They had gotten off the train as it arrived, and started their search for us, believing we were being held hostage.

Renting a car at the station, they had not seen us loading the train. Our disguise had fooled them. They also did not see the Old Fox and Alex, who had been parked around the corner, watching between the buildings with their binoculars as we boarded the train.

The trail of evidence had led them to the mining company.

"There's no one here. Where could they be?" Rico said.

"It's a big mountain; they could be anywhere," Gloria replied, looking through her binoculars.

"They must be here somewhere. The phones don't just go down for no reason," Rico was frustrated.

"If the phones went down, maybe the kids were trying to call home. That would mean the Old Fox and Alex probably cut the phone lines so they could not call! That would mean the kids escaped!" Gloria knew she was on the right track now.

"You're right! Maybe the kids are trying to get home. If they couldn't call, maybe they are trying to get back to Lima."

"But that would mean they might be on the train we just got off, and we did not see them," Gloria was thinking back to the train station, replaying the scene in her mind.

"Maybe we did not see them because they were in disguise, or were planning to stow away."

"That makes sense. They might not have any money, or could not risk telling anyone. Maybe the Old Fox and Alex were on their tail."

"And they would not have seen us if they were not expecting us to be there!" Rico knew they were getting closer.

Their deductive reasoning was interrupted by a call on Gloria's cell phone.

She picked up the call on Zip.

"An explosion? Where?"

"We think the train is okay. We are hoping the kids are on it," Dad said.

"We were just figuring that out, here too," Gloria said.

"We think they are trying to get home, and someone is trying to stop them. They must know something about the terrorist plan."

"If the train is okay, what caused the explosion?" Rico asked.

"A car. We don't have much information yet. Satellite photos picked up the explosion and the wreckage of a car. We are sending Richard in a chopper to investigate."

"Have you talked to the engineer yet?" Gloria asked.

"No, the radio on the train is out. We are hoping that means the kids are still alive, and someone has cut the radio so they cannot call," Dad's voice was cracking with emotion.

"Then, it would mean someone is still on the train. If the car were trying to stop the train, whoever was on it would not have been able to cut the radio. We have to catch that train."

"Gloria, look over here!" Rico called out.

He had spotted the cut in the phone line outside of the Peru Mining Company.

"Let's go! We have a train to catch!" She said, running to the rented car.

The train rolled along while we ate. Other people in the car had taken out their lunches too. The conductor was offering refreshments. He had sandwiches and cold drinks. The engineer was busy trying to get the radio to work. The steady clack of the wheels became a comforting sound in the background, lulling the passengers into a sense of security.

My thoughts were on Lima, and seeing Mom and Dad again. Paolo also was thinking of home.

Maria watched us eat, anxious to talk when we were finished. Her eyes kept going to Paolo when he wasn't looking, and I could see she had a crush on him. I smiled, thinking of Dimitri, the boy I had met in Russia who had a crush on me. I liked Paolo too, and was surprised how I wasn't jealous when I noticed Maria's looks.

Dimitri would have been pleased.

Maria's family was also aware of Maria's attention, but did not seem too concerned. "Just children, nothing to worry about," their eyes said.

Isabella smiled.

There were three cars on this train. We were in the lead car, there was a second car of passengers, and there was a third car with the freight and luggage. It was just a commuter train on a routine trip to Lima.

No one in the second car paid much attention to the man in the back when he stood up and walked to the front of the car.

Wearing jeans and a striped peasant shirt under a woven poncho and a round hat, he looked like many of the natives in Peru. His weathered face had a kind smile showing a few missing teeth. He smiled at people, and they smiled back.

When he reached the door of the car and stepped out, no one thought anything of it.

He stood on the metal platform, and watched the ties fly by underneath. The sound of the wheels seemed to cloak him from sight as he climbed to the back of the first car and opened the door.

Stepping into our car, he quietly shut the door, the sleepy passengers taking the sound for the conductor.

He stood for a moment until he spotted his destination and walked slowly down the aisle, smiling at the few curious looks he received.

Seated across from Paolo and me, Roberto looked up, and saw the friendly stranger. He smiled, nodded, and the man smiled back.

Something sent a chill down my back. I could feel eyes on the back of my head. I wanted to turn and look back, but something in Roberto's manner told me not to.

The chopper landed at the crossing, and Richard climbed out, telling the pilot to wait and keep the motor running.

He examined the wreckage of the car and looked for traces of the occupants.

Climbing back in the helicopter, he told the pilot to take off as he picked up the radio's microphone.

"The kids were not in the car," he told my parents, relieved. "I think they are on the train. We are in pursuit of it now."

Rico held the pedal to the floor, flying along the road at full speed.

"Do you think we can catch them?" Gloria asked.

"We sure are going to try!" Rico replied as he pushed down on the pedal even harder.

Maria looked up, taking her eyes off Paolo for the first time since we had started eating. Little Clarissa looked up, too.

They were smiling at someone.

chapter Thirty-Nine

The smiling man had been sent by The Path. They hadn't liked the Old Fox working alone, and had suspected him of kidnapping us. The plan was too important to them. They had their own reasons for being involved. So they watched without the Old Fox knowing it.

Rico and Gloria might have spotted the man at the train station, but he had seen them first. He had also seen us board the train. Our disguises did not fool him.

He had reasoned we would not be traveling alone, and knowing the Old Fox was looking for us, it was simple deduction we would come to the station.

Now he stood before us with the disarming smile of a simple peasant.

He reached under his poncho and drew a gun, ready to shoot us all.

Rico and Gloria were gaining on the train. "I see it!" Gloria shouted as the car bumped along, kicking up dust on the dirt road.

"We can catch it!" Rico shouted back.

"What do we do then?"

"We stop it!"

"How?"

"I don't know yet," he said, "but we'll think of something."

The helicopter was much faster than the car.

"There it is!" The pilot said.

Richard looked out the window as the copter banked towards the tracks. He could see the train now and something else.

"There's a car chasing it, too.

"What do we do when we catch it?" The pilot asked

"Fly in front of it and get the engineer's attention. Try to get him to stop!"

The pilot nodded and pushed the stick forward.

"Hi, mister," Clarissa said, her big brown eyes catching the smiling assassin.

It was just the hesitation Roberto had hoped for. He jumped out of his seat, arms outstretched, reaching for the gun.

The gun flew as Maria's father landed on top of the would-be killer. They rolled in the narrow aisle as people picked up their feet, surprised at the sudden commotion.

The smiling man rolled on top of Roberto. He drew a knife and was ready to thrust it, when a sharp crack from Isabella's cane crashed into his head!

The knife fell from his hand, and Roberto pushed him off, rolling out from underneath him.

"Miguel, get me some rope! Let's tie him up."

"Who has any rope?" Miguel asked the passengers. "Anything, before he wakes up!"

"I have something!" One of the passengers stood up, holding up his bag. He dug through it, and pulled out a pair of long leather laces for his work boots.

179

Stepping over the lady next to him, he gave them to Miguel, who helped his father wrap them around the smiling man's wrists and feet.

"That should hold him. If he wakes up, hit him with your cane again!"

"Rose! Look out the window!" Paolo shouted. "There is another car!"

"Sheesh. How many killers are after us?" I said

But there was something familiar about the people in the car. "It's Gloria and Rico."

Gloria looked out the car window. Keeping pace with the train, she could see the passengers now. She looked up, and saw me waving and smiling.

"The kids are okay!" She shouted to Rico.

The helicopter finally caught up, and the pilot ignored the speeding car. He flew ahead of the train to give himself room to turn around. Now he flew towards the train as if playing chicken.

The startled engineer shook his head. "What is going on? First the radio, and now this!"

He watched as the helicopter repeated the maneuver, this time seeing the men signaling him to stop the train.

"They want me to stop the train? They must be terrorists! Or robbers! We are close to Lima now and I will not be late!"

He didn't stop even when the conductor burst into the engine with the news of the smiling man.

The train rolled into the station in Lima with a helicopter escort, and the black rental car of Rico and Gloria's in pursuit.

The engineer was met with guns as Dad and Mom and several police descended on the train. He shrugged and looked at his watch.

"Right on time!" He said, smiling.

"Mom! Dad!" I yelled as we herded off the train. Police and security surrounded us. All the passengers were detained and questioned as the press was held back behind hastily-constructed barricades.

"Rose!" They both said together. I could hear the mixed emotions of relief and anger in their voices.

Paolo's father and grandmother were there as well and Rico, Gloria, and Richard were making their way through the crowd.

As much as I was happy to see them, I felt an urgency to tell them what I knew.

I hoped it wasn't too late!

Chapter Forty

Monday morning, every T.V. and radio station in the free world was interrupted with the news of the latest terrorist attack.

"Las Vegas, Nevada. At six a.m. this morning a bomb hidden in an ambulance destroyed several casinos and killed hundreds. Hundreds more were injured. Details are sketchy but those numbers could run into the thousands. The ambulance and its occupants were completely destroyed by the bomb, which experts are saying was nuclear. The danger of radiation may render the city uninhabitable for years! We have cancelled all programming to bring you the story as it unfolds."

It was six-thirty a.m.

While the world listened in shock the president was preparing to face the nation. Picking up the phone, he called the director of the Agency.

"I want every security person available in Vegas, now. And I want you here with me. You are going to explain at the press conference how this could have happened!"

At six forty-five, the president was interrupted by another news bulletin even as his chief of staff rushed into the Oval Office.

"The Golden Gate Bridge has just collapsed!" The news-caster, already in shock from the Vegas disaster was now reporting a second attack.

"No, I can't believe it! The Brooklyn Bridge is gone!" He continued. "Thousands of motorists trapped in their cars have died. The morning traffic jam on both coasts has turned deadly."

Live cameras from helicopters covered the scenes of horror. Cars on fire plummeted into the water as the bridges collapsed. Trucks were thrown into the air, only to land on other cars and roadways, killing more people, and blocking roads in New York, spreading a chain reaction of explosions and crashes that would paralyze the country.

People were paralyzed – frozen in disbelief in front of televisions and radios in every home and workplace. It was as if the whole world had stopped.

The press conference at the White House was a disaster, as both the president and the director of the Agency had no answers for the questions.

"How could this have happened?" one reporter demanded to know.

"Why didn't we see this coming?"

"Are we at war?" another asked.

"What happened to our security?"

On and on the questions went.

"Apparently the attack on Las Vegas was both symbolic, and a decoy. While we focused all of our attention on the disaster there, the terrorists were able to send nuclear car bombs to the bridges. Clearly, their plan is to cripple our economy," the president said.

"We had a special team on the job," the director said. "They were close to discovering the secret terrorist plan, and when they finally did, it was too late."

The director had already made a deal with the president. When it was time for heads to roll on this one, it wouldn't be theirs.

The day wore on into a week as the images were repeated time and time again. Experts appeared from everywhere, explaining their theories, and speculating on how such a massive plan could have been kept so quiet for so long.

The death toll continued to rise. The numbers were staggering.

The economy of the U.S. was near breakdown and the ripple effect was spreading to the European community and the Third World.

Thousands of businesses were closed – some forever – as their staffs had perished in the tragedies.

It was the longest, darkest, day in history -- unless you were a terrorist.

The world sat stunned, waiting for the next terrible announcement.

I would have been glad to see a commercial.

That's what would have happened if Mom and Dad hadn't listened. Fortunately, they did!

At six o'clock on Monday morning, Tony Shiffer left the roadside motel on the way to Vegas. He was almost there. He had managed to save 500 dollars over the last year from the various temp jobs he had held all year in Sioux City, Iowa.

Now he was on his way to Vegas in his old, rusted Buick Skylark. Forty-five and a failure, he would take one more roll of the dice and strike it rich. And if he lost? He didn't want to think about that. There just wasn't anything else to live for.

While he slept, a car rolled quietly into the parking lot. One man dressed in black, wearing a stocking hat walked over to Tony's car. He bent down, and took a package from his pocket.

Silent and quick, he reached under the rusted door panel and found the car's frame. There was a metallic 'click' as the magnetized bomb bonded with the metal. The man stood up and jumped into the waiting car, which drove quietly away. None of the occupants of the motel were awakened.

Tony was hungry and resisted the urge to stop at the truck stop diner. He could eat in Vegas! His plan was to arrive at 6:30.

And he would have, if he had better tires. Somewhere between the motel and Vegas, on an open stretch of road there was an explosion. Tony fought to keep the car on the road as the right front tire went flat from the blowout. He managed to pull the car over to the side.

"Darn! No spare!" He said, looking at the empty trunk. He had already known that, but decided to look for one anyway. Who knows?

Slamming the trunk, he started walking away from the car. Back to the gas station he had seen on the way.

After about fifteen minutes the rest of the tires blew!

"Funny, didn't sound like tires," he thought as the blast knocked him to the ground.

Picking himself up, he looked back in the direction of his car. The small speck he had seen a few minutes ago was gone.

"I got a bad feeling about this," he said to himself as a black Suburban pulled up alongside him.

The dark-tinted window on the passenger side rolled down. There was a man with a high-power rifle.

"Get in!" he said.

Tony didn't argue.

"Sorry about your car. I didn't even get the shot off when the tire blew by itself! Boy, you must have had crappy tires on that thing. You must have an angel too!"

While Tony sat, bewildered, in the back seat, the man opened a laptop computer.

"Steven, the suitcase is closed," he said, and closed the laptop again.

Tony wondered what he had gotten into!

Back at the Ready Room, Steven and Susan high-fived each other! One down, two to go!

"I'm glad you thought of that plan!" Susan said.

"A stroke of luck. After we got the information from Rose, I tried to imagine how they would get a bomb into Vegas. It seemed like the only way. Terrorists are famous for car bombs, anyway. The long-range security would have profiled an operative, and so it seemed logical to choose a random innocent driver and plant a bomb on the car. There weren't too many driving to Vegas so we decided to shoot out a tire here and there."

"Why his car?" Susan asked.

"I don't know. Guess I just don't like old rusted Buicks," Steven said with a wink.

"What about the other two targets?" Susan asked.

"My guess is they will use the same scenario," Steven shrugged.

"Good thing we closed the bridges at four a.m. this morning," Aunt Susan hugged Uncle Steven's arm.

"Yeah, there will be a lot of angry commuters today!" Uncle Steven patted Aunt Susan's hand and smiled down at her.

"Angry, but alive!" Susan said, turning back to Zip.

The split screen showed the two bridges. The liaison from the Agency was on the Brooklyn side. Another agent was on the Golden Gate side.

"The suitcases are packed and ready," they said, reporting in.

"Good. Get ready to meet your travelers!" Susan said.

Chapter Forty-One

But the suitcase wasn't closed! While Tony sat being questioned in the Suburban, emergency vehicles rushed to the scene of the explosion!

Police and security agents combed the area for clues as motorists began stopping for the barricades. Soon, the area was full of people. Reporters rushed to the scene and crowds of spectators had gathered.

One man in a radiation suit held a ground sweeper looking for radiation. It was standard procedure, and so far he had not found any radiation from the bomb in Tony's car.

Satisfied, he shrugged, and made his way back to the perimeter.

It was when he passed the ambulance where Tony was now undergoing examination when the Geiger went off.

"Got something here!" The man said through the radio in his headgear.

"Residual?" The question came back.

"No. Too strong! It's live. I think we have another bomb!"

"Where? What's the source?"

"Seems to be coming from the ambulance!"

"Medical equipment?" The voice asked.

"No. Too strong!" The man in the suit said as he swept the vehicle.

"Get them out!" The voice said.

In seconds, agents descended on the ambulance, herding the crew and Tony into the Suburban.

The police used bullhorns to evacuate the area as the Suburban pulled out, taking the ambulance crew and Tony away for questioning.

Back at the Ready Room, Susan, and Steven were interrupted by a call on Zip.

"The suitcase is still open! I repeat the suitcase is still open!"

"What's happening out there?" Steven asked.

"Apparently, the bomb in Tony's car was a decoy. It was a real bomb, set to go off on signal, but only as an excuse to send in the real bomb, which was hidden in an ambulance. The second bomb is nuclear!"

"My God!" Susan said. "What's the status of the ambulance?"

"The Bomb Squad has already located the bomb, and is diffusing it now. It's small, but deadly."

"Does the crew know anything about it?"

"At this point, neither the ambulance crew nor the driver of the car, seem to know anything about it. We think the bombs were planted without their knowledge. Judging by the one found on the ambulance, both bombs were small packages magnetically attached to the frames of the vehicles," the agent reported.

"Makes sense," Steven said. "Good way to get past our security – unknowing carriers no one would suspect."

"First bomb goes off, send in the ambulance!" Susan said, shivering from the thought.

"My guess is they will use the same plan for all three targets. They have learned from 9/11." Steven speculated.

"Right! With the heightened security since 9/11, they would not risk open communications. That's why the chatter has been so low. Word of mouth passed in code, delaying the wire for more sophisticated computers for the Agency, and using carrier pigeons instead of operatives to deliver the packages! Ingenious! Thank God it didn't work!" Susan sighed.

"Good thing the bridges are closed!" The Vegas agent said.

It was precisely then that two more explosions were reported, one in New York, and one in San Francisco.

The T.V. monitors in the Ready Room showed scenes from both coasts now as reporters followed the new explosions. "Details are sketchy…"

Zips monitor divided into three views covering all three locations. Amazingly, no one was killed in the explosions. Both cars were parked and the streets were littered with debris. Chain reaction fires and explosions from nearby cars and houses continued to rock the neighborhoods.

Apparently, both owners were in their houses when the bombs went off, delaying their morning commute to work with the news that the bridges they normally used were closed.

Steven was talking to both sites at once. "That's right, check all the emergency vehicles! All of them!"

Back in Vegas, the bomb squad had disabled the second bomb.

"Steven, Susan, we have some info on the bomb," the Vegas agent broke in.

"What have you got?" Steven said.

"If it wasn't nuclear we would never have found it. The package contained a low-frequency receiver. It was set to go off on signal; a radio signal," he said, holding up his hands, showing a 9-volt battery, and a small red wire.

The same kind of wire my grandfather had used in his ham radio.

"There's some writing on the wire," he continued.

"What does it say?" Susan asked.

"It says *Peru Wire Company.*"

"Bingo!" Susan said high-fiving Steven's hand.

Chapter
Forty-Two

The fire vehicles were delayed a few minutes as each one was inspected for the hidden bombs. The delay was costly, but necessary.

Eventually, the bomb in Brooklyn was found on the lead fire truck of the closest station. It would have been the first on the scene had the car blown up on the bridge. The nuclear charge was designed to make sure the bridge was destroyed.

A similar scenario was discovered in San Francisco.

Mom and Dad were following the events on T.V. and Zip.

"Apparently, the terrorists were planning on crippling the economy rather than destroying it," Dad was saying.

"Yes, we've thought for a long time they are more interested in 'hit and run' than in a World War, or totally destroying the U.S.A.," Mom added.

"Yeah, truth is, they need us. Much of their funding comes from unsuspecting citizens."

"Not to mention other groups who have a bone to pick with us, or a financial interest in causing chaos."

"Like The Shining Path, the drug lords, and the old hard-line Communists," Dad concluded.

We turned our attention back to the T.V.

"Many people are rushing to churches across the USA and the world today. The president is assuring people we are not at war, and as bad as the attacks were today, they could have been much, much worse. As it is, our agents in the field have been able to short out the second part of the terrorist's plan, which at this point looks like three targets..."

The T.V. suddenly blanked out, causing our heart rates to jump suddenly. When it came back on, the network had gone to commercial.

"Looks like a news blackout." Dad said.

"Yeah, it is an election year." Mom nodded.

"Eventually the whole story will come out. For now the news people have plenty to talk about and cover," Dad said.

"When all the facts are in, they'll put a spin on it," Mom said.

"But that's how it works in the Good Ol' USA!" I said.

Mom and Dad looked at me and smiled.

The next few days were filled with 'official' activity. Mom and Dad took me everywhere as they were interviewed by the Agency and filed their reports.

Paolo went with us along with his father and grandmother. Maria and her family were brought along as well. Rico, Gloria, and Richard were our bodyguards, and a special team was sent to assist them.

We were driven in four separate vehicles for extra security. Every trip was a covert operation.

Paolo and I told our story over and over again. It was fun for a while but soon we got tired of it all.

"Mom, when do we get to go to Machu Picchu?" I asked as we rode in the black limo to the Government Building in Lima.

The leather seats were slippery under the dark blue dress I had been forced to wear. Paolo and his father were in suits and ties and Maria, wearing a white ruffled dress, smiled every time she caught Paolo looking at her.

We were on our way to an unofficial,'official' dinner to honor us all for our part in the foiling the terrorist plot.

This would be a night to remember, and a night we could never talk about. Sheesh!

"Soon, Rose. We'll be staying an extra week, and I promise we'll have our vacation. We'll get to Machu Picchu."

"What about Richard? Will he get to go fishing?"

"Yes, though I don't think he's anxious to get in the water.

Up front, Richard turned around and smiled as the car turned into the drive in front of the government center.

I thought about Sam. Right now I needed somebody to hug.

Chapter Forty-Three

We felt like celebrities on Entertainment Tonight as we stepped out of the limo, and were surrounded by special agents in suits all wearing little coiled wires in one ear.

We were escorted to the dining room in small, separate groups for our safety. The room was full of important-looking people dressed in tuxedos and gowns. The tables were all set with fancy china and glassware on white tablecloths.

There was a round of applause as we walked in, and were escorted to the tables set on the stage. A microphone and podium were set up between the two long tables we were seated at. Above the podium was a large video screen.

I blushed at the applause as it grew to a standing ovation. Paolo bent his head sheepishly as the three sets of parents beamed with pride.

"Ladies and gentlemen, may I present our guests of honor…" the speaker began.

The Vice President of Peru.

I don't remember what we ate, or much about the night. I know I was nervous as I stood at the microphone accepting a plaque from the government of Peru, and an honorary agent status from the Agency.

When all the talking was done, the lights were dimmed and the video screen came to life.

It was the president of the United States! Using a video link with Zip and the cameras in the room, we were able to talk to him.

"Rose, Paolo, and your families, I want you to know you have our gratitude for what you have done to stop the latest terrorist plan. Your families have banded together in this fight, and we have won this round. Because I cannot be there in person we set up this video link and I now present you all with a Congressional Medal of Honor. Unfortunately, for security reasons we cannot make this public. Nor will anyone hear the full story. This is being done for your safety and I ask that everyone in the room agree to the secrecy in all our best interests. Please raise your right hands now to signify your agreement."

Everyone did and the president continued. "We want you to know this investigation has just begun. We will not stop until we know all the details of the plan, and have captured those involved."

There was a round of applause for the president as he signed off, and the lights came up to full.

The local Agency director talked to us as we ate our deserts, telling us the battle for a safe world never stops and how even two young children can make a difference.

There were a lot of introductions, and hand shaking at the end. Finally, we were led back to the cars, and taken to new rooms in the hotel.

Paolo and Maria's families stayed at the hotel also.

Plainclothes men were stationed throughout the hotel and I wondered how long we would be watched.

Alone in our new suite at last, I snuggled on the couch between Mom and Dad.

"Sheesh! That was intense! What's going to happen tomorrow?" I asked.

"Tomorrow, Mom and I have some work to do with the Agency. We will file our reports, and look at participating in the on-going investigation," Dad said, as he removed his bow tie.

"Do you think you'll get more jobs as private contractors?" I asked.

"Well, thanks to you and your shenanigans…" Mom had a serious look on her face, and I began to worry.

"Oh, oh," I said, waiting for the lecture I knew was bound to come, "here it comes!"

"As I was saying," Mom said in a stern voice, "thanks to you and your shenanigans, we have a five-year contract!"

"That is, after our vacation next week!" Dad said, smiling.

"Just remember one thing, Miss Rose…" Mom continued, "just because you are an honorary agent doesn't mean you can go running off with boys anytime you feel like it!" Mom got the lecture in after all.

That night, I slept in my own private room. I said goodnight to Grandpa and Grandma as I always did and thought about Samson the Great.

He'd love this bed!

Chapter
Forty-Four

Eventually, they did find out how the terrorists planted the bombs. It was a simple matter of scheduled maintenance and records kept online.

Using the skills of experienced hackers it was not too hard to get into the computers of the fire companies and the hospitals, and view the maintenance schedules of the vehicles involved.

Knowing when and where the oil changes were done, the terrorists planted a man at the scene. Using fake I.D.s, three Americans sympathetic to the 'cause' were given part-time jobs well ahead of the planned event. Gaining the trust of their employers was easy, and when the vehicles showed up for oil changes they were given something extra.

A small package containing a nuclear device was attached to the inside of the frames where no one would ever see or suspect it. Each contained a small receiver. The receivers were tuned to different frequencies of local ham radios. A small 9-volt battery powered the receiver. At the specified time, a signal would be sent over the hacked into frequency of the ham radio in the area.

Ka-Boom. Down went the bridges and Las Vegas, too!

Of course, by that time, the 'employees' of the oil change garages had moved on, leaving no forwarding addresses or trail. People even forgot what they looked like, but everyone remembered what good guys they were.

The genius of the plan was there would be no operatives in the area when the blasts occurred. No one would be coming or going at the airports, there would be no suspicious movements of those being watched. It would be a complete surprise.

The delay in the wire for the Agency's new computers was for two reasons. First, so the subtle probing into ham radio records at the fire stations and hospital would not be detected, and the procuring of plutonium needed for the bombs would not be traced.

The two-year plan was set up by word of mouth, and passed in code from one cell to another, each being given a part of the plan – but not the whole thing. The bits of code passed in restaurant conversations were too small to be noticed, and under penalty of death each person was sworn to secrecy.

To make up for the funds that would be lost in the disruption of the U.S. economy, interested parties were contacted and invited to participate for a fee: hard-line communists, drug lords, and of course, The Path. Each had a vested interest in striking a blow to the United States.

It all would have worked if Paolo and I hadn't been in the right place at the right time. And, if Alex and the Old Fox had not talked about it when they did. The one mistake in the plan was letting them know what the targets were. Of course, it was necessary to secure their co-operation.

Richard told all of this to Mom and Dad, winking at me when he mentioned Paolo and me.

That brings me back to the rest of the story.

Paolo's little house was full of activity as we all gathered for a farewell lunch. The two grandmothers and Christina were busy in the little kitchen, and Paolo's father took Roberto and Miguel for a ride on his fishing boat. Mom, Dad and Richard were busy setting up the tables and chairs in the back yard as Rico and Gloria served as waiters, running food and beverages to the tables until it was time for everyone to sit down and eat.

Paolo, Maria and I sat on the dock, talking about what would happen next.

"We'll miss you, Rose," Paolo said, his brown eyes tearing up.

"Yes, I will miss you, too," Maria echoed.

"Sheesh! This is supposed to be a celebration! You have got me all choked up. You know I'm going to miss you too!" I said, holding back hot tears.

I sat quiet for a few minutes, watching the fishing boat make its turn and head back for the dock.

"I have something for each of you," I said, reaching into the canvas bag I'd had through everything that had happened.

I pulled out the gifts Mom and I had bought on the plaza; two portable CD players, one red and one blue, and a selection of music to go with each one.

"Which color would you like?" I asked them.

"Rose," Paolo said, taking the blue one. "I have something for you, after we eat."

"Me too," Maria echoed again, taking the red player.

"Okay, but no more crying. We will see each other again. And we can stay in touch. I'm still writing my newsletter on the Internet. You can still send me mail. We will still be friends. Promise?"

So we did as the boat drifted up to the dock. Miguel jumped out to tie it up, beaming from his first ride on the water.

From the house, Paolo's grandmother waved us in.

"Let's eat!"

It was decided Maria and her family would be watched for their safety, and escorted back to Cerro de Pasco. They sold their goods to Paolo's grandmother, who lovingly displayed them in her shop. I proudly carried the hand-embroidered canvas bag, made by Maria's grandmother, with the beautiful Aztec design on the outside. Inside the bag was the gift from Paolo, a hand-carved piece of driftwood in the shape of a rose.

"My father carved it for me after I grew the rose bushes," Paolo explained as he handed it to me, "I wanted you to have it."

So much for my "No More Crying" rule! I smiled as the tears rolled down my cheeks again. I was still crying as we all said goodbye.

Paolo and Maria were seen holding hands as they walked to the train that would take Maria's family home.

Paolo's father returned to his fishing boat, and Paolo returned to working at the hotel.

Rico and Gloria would keep an eye on him and his family.

As for me, I knew I was in a battle for independence.

"What should we do with you, Rose?" Dad said as we rode in the car on our way to Machu Picchu.

"Whatever do you mean, Father?" I said, formally.

"Well, you are now a target of the terrorists as well as the hard-line communists. We may have to send you to a convent!"

"You wouldn't." I gasped the words out.

"Well, it is a thought…" Mom said.

"But, but…" I said, pretending I believed them.

"Actually, both the terrorists and the hard-liners are laying low. Obviously they are working on their next plan, and feel a vengeance strike against any of us would call attention to them. We believe they feel it is safer to just watch us like we watch them. But, it's still a factor we have to consider. Sheesh!" Dad said, sounding like me now.

Richard had been sitting quietly next to me in the back seat through the whole conversation. I looked at him for help.

"Now, you know they won't let me stay in a convent with Rose. I propose we release her under my supervision when you two are gone. I'll keep an eye on her. And don't forget the tutor. She'll be watching too!"

"And don't forget Sam!" I said, hopefully. "And the fact both my parents are agents. And my aunt and uncle, too."

"Well, you have some valid arguments there, young lady. Why don't we make our decision after we see Machu Picchu?" Dad said as he pulled the car into the train station. The train would take us on the six-hour journey to Machu Picchu, where we would stay at the Tourist Hotel overnight. Rico and Gloria had made all of the arrangements, charging the Agency for their services as the Peru Travel Service.

"Okay, sounds like a deal under one condition; Mom has to keep her promise to tell me about how Grandma and Grandpa met in Machu Picchu and show me the wire forest Grandpa told me about."

"Okay, you've got a deal," Mom, said as we opened the trunk to take out our bags.

"It's a good thing Susan and Steven agreed to stay on at the house with Sam, even though their house is finished," Dad said, grabbing his bags.

"They have to stay and help with the investigation anyway," Mom said.

"Well, we finally get our vacation!" I said.

"And I finally get my fishing trip!" Richard smiled.

"See you in a week. Hope you catch the giant red cat-fish!" Dad waved as Richard walked away.

"I will! It's guaranteed in the fee! Oh, by the way, Rose, your suitcase is open."

"What?" I said, ready for action.

"Made you look!" He laughed, disappearing through the doors of the station.

We all laughed as we followed him in.

Epilogue

Mom and I stood on the lookout at Machu Picchu. Below us was the road leading back into the forest, winding through the Andes Mountains.

"Your grandfather met your grandmother on a guided tour right here at Machu Picchu. It was the first time either of them had been here. This lookout is where he told her the story that landed him their first date. The very next day they went into the jungle where he promised he would prove to her his story was true."

"What story did he tell her?" I asked.

"Well, he told her about the wire forests. She was a college student and an archaeologist. She didn't believe a word he said, so of course she had to give him the opportunity to prove it. The next morning they had breakfast together and followed the tour into the rainforest. There they stood, under the canopy looking at the rainbow of colors from all the orchids that grow there. Grandma smiled as he picked one for her, and gave it to her with a wink and a kiss. And that is why she is holding one in her portrait."

There I was standing high on the lookout above the canopy, picturing my grandparents young and in love and imagining the story he had told to win Grandma's heart.

There were tears in my eyes again. Grandpa, you sly old fox. He had won my heart the very same way.

"Come on, young lady, we have to get back. Early day tomorrow," Mom announced.

"Why? Where are we going tomorrow?" I asked.

"Your grandpa wasn't kidding when he told that story," she said with a hint of intrigue.

Dad had stayed behind examining the ruins. He waved as we approached.

The next morning, after breakfast, we followed the tour. Under the canopy of the trees, I saw the orchids and the Wire Forests of Peru.

Partners in life as well as writing, John and Marlene have co-authored many successful works including the *Ramblin' Rose*™ series.

John Carson has been writing since the age of 14. Marlene joined forces with him in 1973 and immediately began to encourage his writing. She became his inspiration and her ideas and expertise proved to be the vital element in creating many of their published works.

Parents and grandparents, they live in St. Cloud, MN.

You can read more about John and Marlene Carson and their works at: **www.readjohncarson.com**

We hope you enjoyed this story. Be sure to check out the rest of the books in *The Ramblin' Rose*™ Series as well as other works by John and other Aspirations Media authors. Your comments and thoughts concerning this book or Aspirations Media are welcome.

www.aspirationsmediainc.com

If you're a writer or know of one who has a work that they'd love to see in print – then send it our way. We're always looking for great manuscripts that meet our guidelines. Aspirations Media is looking forward to hearing from you and/or any others you may refer to us.

Thank you for purchasing this Aspirations Media publication.